I0723334

What Came After

a novel by
Tabor Millien

Briley & Baxter Publications | Plymouth, Massachusetts

ISBN: 978-1-954819-86-3

Book Design: Amy Deyerle-Smith

For my grandparents
Rosa and Calvin
Who I believe will always find each other
No matter what comes next

The whole time the main character of the movie thought the noises and the objects moving around when she wasn't looking were the work of a ghost. Until the man barreled his way through the wall. He was hiding away, living within them for years. Now he was out and murdering her abusive ex-boyfriend who had tracked her down to force her to come back with him.

Then he looked at her. A porcelain doll mask obscured his face, but she could see and feel his eyes locking on hers.

She tried to run but ended up cornered and steeled herself to face him. His head tilted innocently as he looked at her like a quizzical child, but his hairy, dirty, bloody body countered that gesture grotesquely. His breath was loud behind the mask as he leaned into her.

"What does it say about me that this sort of turns me on?" I ask Jules, cuddled up next to him in bed as we watch the scary movie.

"Says you're bat-shit crazy. I been telling you that for years though," he replies with a lopsided grin.

"Whatever, you jerk," I say and push at his shoulder playfully. I try to scoot away from him, but his arm is already around me to pull me back in.

"Never said I didn't like it," he whispers in my ear as he nuzzles his face against my cheek. He starts trailing kisses down my neck, but I push his face back towards the TV. "Ah, come on Hannah," he protests. "You said you were getting all hot and bothered. Just trying to help you out."

I let him turn my head and give me a kiss but pull away before he deepens it. "The movie probably has like ten minutes left. You can wait," I tell him and turn back to the screen. He sighs, but settles back down to finish watching.

Julien, AKA Jules, has been my boyfriend for four years. We got together our junior year of high school. He was the bad boy of our school. Everyone knew no one messed with Jules – not even the football players, who were always the hotshots of the class.

I was always fascinated by him, and by junior year I was tired of my pathetic life and status as one of the invisibles. For most of my life it was always me and Bobbi. We lived next door to each other and became fast friends. We'd watch true crime shows, ghost hunting shows, gory horror movies, anything taboo we could get our hands on. We'd go out walking at night to the cemetery and peer at the remnants of life, from the old bones beneath our feet to the words etched onto the stones marking where they laid – Loving Mother; Beloved Son; Our Angelic Daughter.

But I got tired of our monotony, so I didn't hesitate ditching Bobbi when I finally caught Jules' attention. I had already begun pulling away from her, trying to detach myself from our lonesome, pathetic duo. I went to a party one night without her, aimlessly wandering around some classmate's house with a red cup in my hand. I noticed Jules and tried to stay in his line of sight. We caught each other's eyes several times, but neither of us made a move.

Some jock tried to hit on me while I was dancing. He grabbed my ass and, when I whirled around to face him, snaked his arm around my waist and pulled me tight against him. I jerked my knee up into his crotch, but he took me down with him when he fell. I punched him square in the nose, and Jules was right there when I stood up. He took my hand gently and brushed his thumb along my knuckles. "I think you may have bruised them with that punch," he said. "You shouldn't hit directly on the knuckles. Maybe I can show you one day."

Of course I took him up on that offer. We sped away on his motorcycle, and I was glued to his side from that moment on.

After the movie, with our limbs entangled under the sheets and that blissful after-sex warmth leading us both towards sleep, Jules starts giggling to himself. My head is on his chest, and I feel it rising and falling in time with the rumbling of those deep, mirthful giggles escaping his body. I don't sit up because I love physically feeling another person's laughter, but I maneuver my head to look up at him.

"What's got you in a giggle fit?" I ask, poking his ribs in the one spot I know he's ticklish.

He swats my hand away and answers, "Thinking I could easily find a mask like that if you want to try something a little different one night, since you're apparently so turned on by men in masks."

I scoff at him and chuckle, but the thought has some merit. To mess with him, I turn my head away from him and say, "That's a great idea. I've been thinking about putting a paper bag over your head, but a mask would work too."

"Hey!" he protests. He grabs some of my hair and pulls it to make me look back at him. I can't hide the smile creeping across my face. "You're mean as hell, you know that?" he asks and flicks me on the forehead.

That makes me sit up.

"Ugh! You know I hate when you do that," I complain, rubbing my forehead.

He rolls his eyes at me causing me to scowl harder. "Don't be a baby. I didn't do it that hard."

I just reply with a *hmmph*, lay on my side turned away from him, and switch off my lamp.

I hear him sigh and settle down next to me. His arm snakes its way around my waist and up to cup my breast. "I could make it up to you."

I pinch his arm. "Keep your junk on your side of the bed. You know I have class early tomorrow." He grumbles *fine* and gives my boob one last squeeze before turning over to let me go to sleep.

Within minutes, I notice the slowing of his breath as he drifts off. I lay there beside him wondering, not for the first time, if this is how I envisioned our life together. I also continue the debate I've been having with myself about whether or not to pull down the façade and tell him more about my past.

But I gave up friends. I gave up interests. I constructed a new personality. That's who he fell in love with, isn't it? If I take off the hot, popular girl mask and reveal my goofy, dorky, macabre-obsessed mind, would he still want me?

Once again, I'm at an impasse with myself. I am no closer to making a decision, and I can't fight my fatigue any longer. I drift off to sleep with questions about my identity swarming in my mind.

I wake up early the next morning feeling like I only just fell asleep, but drag myself out of bed anyway to go to my classes at our local community college, which is always fully enrolled with the graduating class of our small, mountainside town's high school. Everybody gravitates toward it for multiple reasons: saving money and getting credits that would transfer to somewhere bigger and better; convenience; or following our parents' money (which is my case).

After succeeding at not falling asleep in any of my classes, I meet up with Christine and Shelley in the commons area–a small grassy square with sparse trees, a couple of benches and table or two the school was built around so that, even when you are having your nature break, you are still surrounded by the school on all sides. Even so, I enjoy lingering around the commons between classes – especially this time of year. It's just starting to get chilly. The mountain is coated with snow but we haven't gotten any yet and probably won't for another month. It's pleasant during the day, but getting colder each night.

As I chat with my friends, Bobbi and her boyfriend, Mark, start walking across the commons. Bobbi and Mark got together at the beginning of the year. She's been going to church with him, which I find ridiculous considering the conversations me and Bobbi used to have about religion, life after death, and the paranormal. Basically, it boiled down to: religion is dumb because no one knows. Why should you structure your life around rules that some random group of nobodies way back when decided is how you have to live in order to get into Heaven? Especially when Heaven cannot possibly be proven to be a real place you go after death. Especially when it is way more plausible that our existence was a huge *huh, how did that happen?* from the universe and, since our existence was not specially planned, our death wouldn't be either. There are just too many what ifs, so fretting over it and basing your life and future around it is ridiculous. If you waste your time thinking so far ahead, you'll miss all the fun now. That was our thinking back then, and I've held strong to those beliefs. Bobbi, on the other hand, seems to have caved at the first sign of interest from a guy.

Basically what I'm saying is I don't like Mark. And even though I removed Bobbi from my life, I'm disappointed in her for switching her tune so quickly for him. So, of course, I can't let them have their nice moment in the sun before heading back into the dreary college hallways.

I call out, "Hey Mark, how's the forty-year virgin challenge going?"

When I say Mark is religious, I mean majorly religious. Which isn't necessarily a bad thing in general, but he's the type who shoves his beliefs down your throat. The type who preaches about Jesus's love then, in almost the same breath, call someone the f-slur while yelling at them about how they are going to spend eternity burning in hell. That goes for people who have premarital sex too.

"Maybe someone like you couldn't possibly understand, but our relationship is so much more special without sexual intercourse," Mark argues back, his voice getting higher and his face redder as he goes on. "We truly care about each other on a deep, spiritual level and nothing you could possibly spew from your vile mouth could change that!"

"Testy, testy!" I click my tongue. "Love thy neighbor, Mark. That's one of the big ten. Don't want to disappoint you know who," I say with a nod to the sky. My friends snigger behind me.

"Come on Mark, let's get to class," Bobbi says sweetly and tugs his arm, not even acknowledging me in the slightest. Mark stops glaring at me and lets Bobbi steer him towards the door. I notice his face already losing that angry red hue as Bobbi strokes his arm.

However doting Bobbi is to Mark, it seems to me that she isn't completely satisfied with their arrangement. Bobbi used to always have her fiery red hair cut short, either in a bob or a pixie cut. In order to please Mark, she's let her hair grow out so the ends kiss her shoulders, but she also dresses like the stereotypical fantasy of a schoolgirl. She wears thin shirts with loose cardigans, short skirts, and thigh high socks. Today, her hair is tied up in a tight, neat bun atop her head with her bangs framing her round, innocent-looking face.

"That's quite a cute skirt Bobbi, but it's so short. You should be careful wearing stuff like that around dear Mark. Your ass is hanging out. Don't want to tempt him now, would you?" I say.

Christine and Shelley howl with laughter behind me.

Mark comes whirling back around to lecture me again, but Bobbi doesn't even turn her head a fraction of an inch in my direction. She lets Mark tear away from her and continues inside the building on her own.

"You have serious problems, Hannah. Honestly, you disgust me," Mark says.

I shake off Bobbi's indifference and turn to Mark with the sweetest smile I can muster. "You gonna pray for me, Mark?"

He grimaces and answers, "You need more than my prayers to save you."

fter school, Christine and Shelley follow me to the restaurant where I work. Since weekdays are always slow for business, I'm on the bar this evening. The manager rarely leaves his office, so I stay near them and have a drink or two myself as we chat.

Until a man comes in and sits at the other end of the bar.

I groan and roll my eyes at the girls before I put on my customer service smile and go to take his order. He's looking over the menu when I reach him. I ask my normal, "Would you like a drink to start off with, sir?"

When he looks up at me I realize it's Dale, the man who used to live across the street from my mom.

When I was little, maybe around five years old, my dad left my mom. I didn't see much of him throughout my life. Dale sort of tried to anchor himself in the role of father. I didn't mind him being around so much when I was little because it sort of did fill that newly-opened void, and I thought my mom seemed happier when he was around. But, once I started getting older, his attention towards me made my skin crawl.

At some barbeque get together we were having at our house when I was twelve, he came up behind me, put his hands on my shoulders, and said, "There's my sweet pea," like he always greeted me. I was getting tired of it at that age. I shrugged my shoulders to get his hands off. "You know I don't like when you call me that anymore," I whined.

His hands slipped from my shoulders down to my hips. He wrapped his arms around my stomach and pulled me tightly against him. I knew whatever he was doing was wrong, and I tried to squirm away but that only made him hold tighter, his breath quickening. I froze when I felt him pushing something against my back. "But you are my sweet pea," he whispered in my ear.

He let me go when one of the other guests opened the door to come inside. I ran to my room and locked myself in for the rest of the party. Once everyone left, my mom convinced me to open the door and tell her what was going on. I wept as I told her because I thought I had done something wrong. She went into a rage alright, but not against me.

Dale never entered our house again, though eventually he apologized to both of us saying he had been in a dark place and was disgusted with himself. He had "found God," he proclaimed, and asked our forgiveness—which we gave. We were friendly with him on the street, but still never invited him over or accepted invitations to dinners at his house. After moving in with Jules I hoped I would run into Dale less, but he came to the restaurant fairly often.

The memory always came when I saw him. I try to shake it off. My customer service smile falters, but I ask again, "Anything to drink?"

"Whiskey on the rocks. Doctor says I shouldn't anymore, but we can keep it between us," he says with a wicked looking grin. He winks at me and continues, "Also would like a burger, rare."

"Fries or chips?"

"Fries sound good, Doll."

My back stiffens at the pet name. He hasn't tried that in quite some time. I shuffle to the kitchen window and hand the cook his order. When I bring him his drink, he asks, "How've you been, Hannah?"

"Quite alright, Mr. Dale. Sorry, I don't have time to chat. I've got to get back to my other customers."

He looks over my shoulder at Christine and Shelley as I turn to walk away. He grabs my arm before I can take a step, and I feel his thumb start a stroking motion. I yank my arm away and turn my head back toward him.

"I just wanted to say, it's good to see you doing so well for yourself. You've turned into quite the woman." His gaze leaves my eyes to wander down my back but quickly locks back on my face. "And please, just call me Dale."

He speaks slow and with a heavy southern drawl that grates on my nerves.

"Yeah, okay. Thanks, Dale," I say, already walking away.

"Jesus, Hannah. You look pale. Line up three shots for us, looks like you need one," Shelley says as I slump against the bar in front of them.

"With pleasure," I grumble. I line up the shot glasses and stretch to get the really good vodka from the top shelf. As I turn back around to pour the shots, I notice Dale staring at me. He tips his glass to me and takes a swig. I shudder but manage to fill each glass without spilling. We click them together, and I gratefully down mine. I breathe out a sigh at the burn in my throat and the warmth spreading across my chest.

"There we go," Shelley smacks the bar. "Looking nice and rosy again."

"Thanks, that guy just gives me the creeps," I tell them.

They aren't discreet at all as they look him over and snigger about his appearance and how he's at the bar alone. I realize I don't really care if he notices them.

"Yeah, looks like a real weirdo," Shelley agrees.

"Oh my God, you know who he looks like?" Christine asks and pauses for dramatic effect. "That dude from Texas Chainsaw Massacre. The dad, ya know?"

"Oh. Em. Gee. Stop it, Christine," Shelley barks with laughter and slaps Christine's shoulder.

"Just saying," Christine giggles. "Really though, Hannah. He's just a nobody. Don't let him see you getting all shook over anything he says. That's probably how he gets off."

"That's sick!" Shelley says and mimics sticking her finger down her throat. "I don't want that image in my head, Christine."

"I wasn't picturing it, you freak," Christine says in a mocking tone and pinches Shelley's thigh.

The bell rings, announcing Dale's food is ready. I am determined to show Dale and the girls that he doesn't shake me. I pick up his plate and slide it a bit noisily onto the bar in front of him. I immediately turn to walk away. I hear a "Thank you, Hannah," to which I reply with a curt "Sure," already half way to the other side of the bar.

"Yes, bitch! That's how you fucking do it!" Christine cheers.

We continue to gossip and joke around as usual after that. Dale is completely forgotten by Christine and Shelley, though I still catch him out of the corner of my eye staring. I doubt they notice when he leaves, but I feel much more relaxed without his presence bearing down on me.

After he leaves, Bobbi and Mark come up. She pops up as I'm wiping down the bar. I wasn't expecting to see her here, but what really catches me off guard is the sincere, worried look in her eyes as her hand reaches out to gently hold mine. "Are you okay, Hannah? I saw him. At the end of the bar."

Bobbi knows all about Dale. Back in the day, there was nothing we wouldn't tell each other. Bobbi is the only person who knows all my secrets; that didn't change just because I ditched her. She still knows me better than anyone else. Being her friend and accepting her comfort, though, isn't part of my life anymore. I catch Christine and Shelley glaring at us out of the corner of my eye, so I snatch my hand back and scoff. "Him? Please, he's just a nobody."

Christine picks up her drink and walks over to us. She pretends to catch her foot on one of the bar stools and throws her drink all the way down Bobbi's shirt. "Oh shucks! Clumsy Christine, huh? Sorry Bobbi. Guess you should cut me off, Hannah."

Mark scrambles to Bobbi's side but before he can say anything, Shelley's shrill laughter starts. She points at Bobbi and says, "Mark, avert your virgin eyes. Your pure Bobbi isn't wearing a bra."

Now everyone's eyes are pulled to Bobbi's chest. It's true. With her thin, billowy shirt now soaked through and stuck to her chest, you can see it clearly. Mark's face flushes, and he hurries to get their jackets from the table.

"Hannah, would you happen to have another towel behind the bar?" Bobbi asks. We look at each other for a moment, and I have the feeling this is a final test. A final chance for me to make amends. A final chance to take the hand she has kept extended all these years, waiting for me to accept and return to the way we had always been.

"Yeah, Hannah," Christine says in her false-sweet voice, cutting through my thoughts like an arrow. "You should give her something to cover up with." I watch Christine smirk at Bobbi and then back at me.

I brace myself, mirror her sly smile, and turn to Bobbi with a shrug. "I'm all out. Bad luck, Bobbi."

Bobbi only stares at me, a look of resignation flooding her eyes. Mark returns and shoves a cardigan in her hands. She finally looks away from me as he pulls her towards the door.

With Christine and Shelley's laughter ringing in my ears, I reach down to one of the shelves behind the bar and place my hand against the stack of dish towels kept there. I grasp them, breathe out slowly for five seconds, then let them go.

3

Despite the fact it was a slow day at work, I'm still exhausted when I make it home. The extensive cleaning and straightening up for closing is always tedious, but I'm feeling more of an emotional exhaustion – which might explain my short temper at finding Julien at home. He had told me that morning he would be working the night shift, yet he sat on the couch playing his video games instead. I storm over and yank the plug for the console out of the wall.

"What the hell, Hannah?" Julien groans.

"I was going to ask the same thing," I shoot back. "What the hell are you doing home?"

"Jeez, thought you might have been happy to see me. Remember when you used to like coming home to me?"

"Don't play dumb. You know why I'm pissed that you're here. Why aren't you at work? I swear to God, if you tell me you ditched, I will kill you."

"I didn't ditch, alright? I was like five minutes late, and the boss flipped out. He said he was tired of my unprofessionalism so I should just go home and don't bother coming back ever again."

My head starts to throb, the beginnings of a migraine creeping up on me. I press my fingers against my closed eyes and try to slow my breathing before I completely lose control. Between gritted teeth I say, "You're saying you were fired. Again."

There's no question in my voice, but he answers with a shrug. "Basically."

"Why can't you commit to a job for more than five goddamn months?" I yell. "My income is not enough for us to pay all our bills! How many times do I have to tell you this to get it through your thick skull?"

"Hannah, just chill. I'll find something else. I'll go looking tomorrow," he says. He moves to pick up his controller again which makes me snap. I snatch it just before he can grab it and throw it against the wall. "Jesus, Hannah!" he yells, finally showing some actual anger instead of his usual bored, tolerant reactions to my nagging. "You seriously have issues! I told you, I'll find another goddamn job!"

An animalistic urge to go on a rampage and break everything in sight grips me, but I clutch my hair in my fists instead and let out a loud UGH before storming off to take a shower so hot I'll look sunburnt when I got out.

After my shower, I head for the kitchen and notice the back door is wide open. My anger had dampened to a simmer but now it flares up again. I slam the door shut and continue on to the kitchen where Julien is already eating a sandwich, knowledgeable enough to realize I'm too angry to make him anything.

"Why did you leave the back door open, idiot? It's freezing," I complain.

"I didn't go outside. It must have been you. I guess you were too focused on tearing me apart as soon as you walked through the door that you didn't even shut it."

"I came in through the front door, dumbass. I swear you lose braincells daily," I say, opening the door to the refrigerator to look for food and get him out of my eyesight.

"You are such a bitch sometimes," he yells. He pushes the refrigerator door hard. I jerk backwards so it won't hit me and turn to glare at him.

The words I'm ready to throw at him like daggers catch in my throat when I see a towering form lurching forward behind Julien.

"Watch out!" I yell and point behind him. It takes him a second to realize I'm not yelling at him about the refrigerator door so, when he turns around, the intruder is already bringing his weapon down towards his head. He tries to get his arm up to block the blow, but it's too late.

Glass flies everywhere as the bottle connects with Julien's head, and I remember his routine of having a beer every night with dinner. I watch his legs crumple beneath him and hear a crunch as he falls face first onto the tile. I scream his name and almost go to kneel beside him before the intruder's lower half comes into view, stepping over Julien's unconscious body. My eyes shoot up, and I take in details lightning quick before turning to run. He's wearing heavy-duty clothes, like what you would wear to go hunting or hiking in the mountains during winter. His boots look especially heavy, likely steel toe. The most peculiar thing, though, is the mask he's chosen to wear. It's one of those silicone ones that go fully over your head, and it was a plain but creepy baby face.

He barrels through the bedroom door just as I swing it shut. I go for the window, but he grabs my hair and yanks me back. His other arm wraps around my waist and tightens like a boa constrictor. He lifts me and throws me on the bed. He climbs on top of me, putting all his weight on my legs so I can't kick. I try to punch him, but he grabs my arms and quickly zip-ties me to the bedpost.

I hear Julien before I see him. What I see is just a blur of the both of them falling to the ground. What I hear is a guttural snarling and something like a war cry. It's the angriest sound I've ever heard in my life but it fills me with relief. He isn't dead, and he will save me.

The two of them tumble around for what feels like hours but was probably only five minutes before Julien is able to jump to his feet. His nose is coated in blood, and he breathes heavily from his mouth. The man gets up too. His mask has fallen off, but he is wearing a ski mask as well. They each throw a few punches before the man tackles Julien.

I hear a lot of grunting from Julien, but they are at the foot of the bed so I can't see them. I keep calling his name desperately. The man stands, drags Julien up only to toss him against the wall, then makes sure to face him toward me. Julien is laid on his side, hogtied, breathing heavily, obviously exhausted and in pain. When he sees me tied to the bed with panic etched on my face, he takes a deep breath and begins to struggle against his bonds.

The man stops by the foot of the bed to retrieve his mask. He pulls it back over his head and climbs on top of me. Watching Julien squirm frantically while feeling the man's hands on my body makes me let out the sob I've been trying to hold back. My tears fuel Julien's rage. He calls the man every rotten name he can think of. The anger and helplessness on Julien's face is painful, but the knowledge that nothing will stop this man hurts much more. I shut my eyes to both of them and try to find a quiet place in my mind I can escape to, but I can't run from the fear coursing through me. The man grabs my face and turns my head to look at him. I hear his breath echoing in the mask, but thankfully can't feel it on my face.

"Open your eyes. I want you to look into my eyes," he says. I shake my head, but his hand envelopes my throat and begins to squeeze. "Open your eyes, or I swear I'll kill you right now." His hand tightens even more causing my brain to go into panic mode. I do as he says, and the pressure eases enough for me to suck in a gulp of air.

I can see the man's eyes through the slits in the mask. They look familiar, but I'm too panicked to think straight. "Why are you doing this?" I whisper.

"Come now, Hannah. I'm only giving you what you wanted. Isn't a man in a mask your fantasy?" he answers. I can tell he's trying to make his voice silky and seductive, but it reminds me of Kaa from Jungle Book.

The implications of his words take a second to dawn on me. I go cold when I realize he's referring to the conversation me and Julien had the night before. "How did you—" I start to ask.

"We don't have time to discuss that," he cuts me off. "I'm almost tempted to let him watch the show, but I think it's best if we leave and find a more private place."

I'm confused for a second about who he's referring to, still reeling at the possibility that someone has been stalking me. Had they just been standing outside listening, or had they somehow gotten a mic in the room? Or a camera? The thought sends chills down my spine. My horrifying musings are broken when I realize the man is heading toward Julien again.

"No, please! Leave him alone!" I beg.

Julien is still snarling and spitting and cursing at the man despite his vulnerable position.

"Don't worry, Hannah," the man sighs. "As much as I would love to bash his head in for good, I can hold back. I know you'd never forgive me if I killed him, but we need a head start. I have to be sure he won't call for help before we gain some ground."

As I struggle against my restraints, I watch Julien struggling against his. Every muscle in his body is taught and strained, until the man deals him a quick kick to the head. Julien goes limp and his string of curses cease. All I can hear now is my own desperate whining.

The man turns back to me and comments on my tear-streaked face. "I promise he'll be alright. Now, you have to go to sleep so I can take you somewhere more private."

He pulls out a needle and a vial from one of his many jacket pockets. He fills the needle and kneels over me again. Holding my face with one hand, he turns my head to the side until my neck is straining. Up until this point I've been trying to keep my sobs silent, not wanting to give him the satisfaction of hearing my distress. However, when the needle enters my neck, a sob wrenches its way out and then I can't hold back any longer. I beg for my life. I beg until the room starts to blur and my head starts to spin. Before I'm submerged in total darkness, I think I hear a whispered, "Just go to sleep, my sweet pea."

He's taking me into the mountains. I'm slumped in the passenger seat of his rickety old truck, listening to its creaking and wheezing as we crash along the mountain trails. I come to slightly when he hits a jolt in the road, whether running over tree limbs or pot holes, but I can't hold on to reality. It's like I'm standing on a snowy slope that's sliding away under my feet. There's nothing to hold on to. I'm trying so hard to trek back to consciousness because I know if I don't fight, no one will find me in these mountains. But the damn slope. The ground keeps slipping away, the snow keeps pushing me back, the snow is blinding, and the thoughts ....

I think of Julien and the last words I spoke to him, so harsh. I replay the sight of him tied up, straining so hard against his restraints to try to get to me, and how quickly his limbs went limp as the man who took me knocked him out. I think of him coming to, confused at first and then full of panic. How long will it take him to get untied? How long until he calls for help? How long until they come looking for me?

Not in enough time to do any good.

I think of what might await me at whatever nook in the mountain this rodent of a man sniffs out. Will I feel it? Because all I feel now is exhaustion from plodding up a mental landslide.

Turns out, I don't feel a thing. I'm too numb from the cold, having been carried through piercing wind and laid down in the snow in only the athletic shorts and the tank top I usually sleep in. All I experience are in short snippets of consciousness:

The truck comes to a staggering stop. My door opens and lets in the bitter chill. His calloused hands grab me by my arms and scoop under my legs. Carrying me to my rest.

The biting snow seeps through my thin shirt. Then it's off, and the snow drills into my flesh.

The sky is black satin with a scattering of pinprick stars. Snow falls into my eyes but I don't mind. I don't want to close them again. I can finally see.

A slight twinge of pain below my stomach and heavy breathing in my ear.

The man kneels over me with only his ski mask on now. His face so close I can touch it. My limbs finally awaken, finally receive the messages from my brain. My arm slowly, still sluggish, reaches up and removes the mask. Him. Oh...

The smell of whiskey as he breathes on me. He whispers, "I'm sorry," against my lips. Though I can't feel his lips brushing mine, I know they are. A shiver of disgust.

Something in his hand. Hurling toward my face.

Complete

And

Utter

Blackness.

I float along a river of silky darkness, my body so relaxed it seems like I don't even have one. I take some solace in the fact it's over. Everything is quiet. My brain is no longer hounding me to get moving, begging me for something new and exciting. I'm nowhere, with nothing to do, seemingly nobody to do anything with even if I wanted to, and I'm glad.

It's all over now, I think.

The soft sound of rushing water is suddenly interrupted by an insistent buzzing which grows louder until it completely obscures the sounds of my river. Then I see a pinprick of light. It quickly grows and rushes toward me. I want to stay in the comforting darkness, but I can't look away from it. It's following me, like the light is inside my eyes so no matter where I look, it's still barreling towards me. Then it surrounds me and I'm blinded by a sharp whiteness.

The light shrinks until I find myself staring at an overhead bulb, buzzing with electricity. Two people with surgical masks obscuring their faces lean over me with knives in hand. I yelp and swat at them as I spring into a sitting position, but my hands go right through them.

I test again, just to make sure I'm not hallucinating.

I pass my hand right through one of their heads. I jump off the table I was laid on. I keep my back turned until I can take a few deep, steadying breaths, then I turn to look.

I wouldn't have been able to identify the body lying on the table as myself by looking at the face alone. Fallen apart in some places, bruised and swollen in others. The shock of seeing the damage makes me forget how to breathe. I must look like a fish, bug-eyed, opening and closing my mouth until I remember how to gulp in air again.

I can recognize my body though, despite the eerie blue tint to the skin. My golden-brown hair seems dimmer and more brittle than usual, but it still hangs down past my shoulders stopping just above my breasts. Seeing myself so broken and exposed makes me suddenly insecure. I want to turn away but can't gather the strength to move even an inch.

"Frozen post-mortem, no frostbite. She couldn't have been out there long before death," I hear one of the doctors say. The other quickly jots it down on the report attached to the clip board cradled in his arm. "Look at this section of hair that's shorter than the rest. That was deliberately cut." Again, the quick scribbling of pencil on paper.

I watch, horrified, as they begin the process of removing my organs. My head is screaming for me to turn away, throw up, run out the door, but I feel rooted to the spot. I can't move my eyes even an inch in another direction. I also notice that I don't feel the need to throw up—I don't feel any sort of physical sensations except for a persistent chill.

"Hannah, you don't have to watch," I hear from behind me.

I turn around slowly to face whoever spoke, then pause to take in the details. He's lanky and looks to be around six feet tall. His hair juts out in various angles, a mass of curls and cowlicks. I believe I heard a hint of a Spanish accent when he spoke, but I can't guess just by looking at him.

"You can see me?" I ask once I remember how to speak, which

takes a few seconds.

"I sure can, Hannah," he replies and smiles warmly at me.

"How do you know my name?"

He points to the table behind me. "It's all over the news and everyone in the town is talking about what happened."

"Okay, how can you see me?"

"I'm dead too," he replies with a shrug, as if it was no big deal.

After a moment of processing this information, I ask, "So, are you like my guide or something? Are you here to usher me to whatever comes next?"

"I don't think so," he answers. Up go his shoulders again. "I haven't really figured out the whole 'moving on' bit myself. I've been here in whatever this is for a while though, so I could show you the ropes at least." He sends another beaming smile my way but I'm not too comforted by his words.

"You've been stuck in this building for how long?"

"Oh no, not here exactly. Just in general, whatever this—" his hand flutters around his head, "—plane of existence is. Limbo or what have you. I was actually in Memphis, but I had this feeling like there was somewhere I needed to be. It feels like what I can only imagine a fish feels when they are hooked and reeled in. It's a pull in your gut, and, if you follow it, it takes you where you need to be. This time I ended up here. And I met you!" Another smile.

He is insatiably cheerful for a dead guy.

"Look, this may all be familiar to you, but I was just murdered so could you please tone down your enthusiasm and give me a minute?"

The smile disappears instantly from his face, and I immediately feel guilty about it. Sadness doesn't seem to fit him well.

"Of course, I'll be quiet and wait for you right here."

I nod a thank you, and he nods back before leaning against the door and studying the ceiling. I turn back to the table and watch silently as the doctors finish and stitch me back up. Good as new, I think bitterly, as I avoid looking at my damaged face.

Once they remove my body from the examination room, I go back to the guy waiting at the door. "You know my name, but I know nothing about you. Tell me a few things."

"Ah, of course," he smiles hesitantly and rubs his palm across his forehead. "I should have introduced myself before. My name is Arthur Mancini, but just call me Art. Everyone I knew always called me Art. The nickname got me interested in painting. I was decent at it. My mom's mom was from Columbia and my dad was from Italy, so I definitely know how to cook. I've got two siblings, both moved away and had families of their own. So uh, yeah, now you know more about me than I do you." He starts rubbing the back of his neck, but his smile is getting more natural again.

I try to smile back. It feels weak but it still brightens his face, and his hand falls back to his side. "Any clue as to what I'm supposed to do now? I mean, why are we still here? Is it because we died young or violently?" I look at him a bit sheepishly. I want to know what happened to him, but he didn't include that information in his introduction so I don't want to force him to tell me.

His eyes soften, and he takes a few steps closer to look into my eyes more directly. "I really wish I could give you all the answers. I can't imagine how hard this is for you. Me, I knew I was dying long before it happened, for a little over a year actually. You, though, no one deserves what you went through."

I have the overwhelming feeling that I will start to bawl my eyes out, but there's no pressure behind my eyes from a build-up of tears waiting to be released. Still, my lip quivers, which I try to hide by turning away. I clear my throat and ask, "All the ghost hunting shows I used to watch with—" a sigh escapes my mouth instead of Bobbi's name. Regrets. I suppose I will have to face a lot of those now. I continue without correcting myself, "They all mentioned unfinished business. Could that be it? Why I'm still here?"

"It certainly could be," Art answers. "We could start with the obvious. Do you know who killed you?"

Anger smothers all other emotions in my head as the memory of pulling off the mask and seeing Dale's face plays behind my eyes. His rancid whiskey breath is seared into my nostrils. The audacity of his tears, pained expression, and worthless apology as he hurtled a rock into my face.

I didn't answer him, but Art must see my anger and gather that I do indeed know. "That seems like a yes to me."

"So, what? I'm just supposed to wait around here until Dale gets caught? What am I gonna do about it when no one can see or hear me?"

"Seeing that Dale gets the justice he deserves is most likely part of it, but there could be other things you need to do. You didn't get to say goodbye to anyone. There may be things you need to let go of."

"If doing those things worked, would you still be stuck here?" I snap at him. Seeing his face fall again makes all the anger drain out of me. I slump against the wall and apologize. "Sorry, I'm just angry. I shouldn't be taking it out on you."

He comes and leans next to me. Our arms rest against each other, but no warmth passes between us. After a beat of silence, Art says, "Like I said before, I really wish I had all the answers for you. I'm sure there are things each of us will have to figure out for ourselves, but I just want you to know you aren't alone in this. We can do it together."

I look up at him to see a smile lift the corners of his mouth once again. "You are one cheerful guy," I say. His smile only grows wider. I feel my lips twitch into a sad smile, trying to mirror his optimism, but it doesn't stick. I shut my eyes and try to remember the feeling of peace I had felt when I was drifting down that dark river before I was made to come back.

I sigh and complain, "I'm cold."

There's a beat of silence before Art replies, and there is more sadness in his voice than I have heard from him this whole conversation. He simply says, "I know."

I plan to wait with my body until the funeral tomorrow. That's the best I can do strategy-wise at the moment. I don't feel like I'm ready to face anyone, no matter if they can see me or not. I would see every regret I had reflected back to me in their eyes and the tears that fell from them. Every tear would be a reminder that, soon enough, that's all that would be left of me—memories that draw forth nothing but sadness and pain. Because how will anyone be able to think of me without thinking of what happened to me in the end? And if eyes are the windows to the soul, perhaps the only glimpses I'll get of the world I so desperately wanted to explore will be through a lens of grief. What kind of exploration would that be?

Art must see how deep in thought I am and guess it could be about nothing good, so he tries to distract me. "I told you a bit about me. It's your turn. Tell me about Hannah King."

Still feeling forlorn and pessimistic, I reply, "She was a bitch. You would have hated her."

There's a beat of silence, so I cock my head to the side just enough to peek over at him out of the corner of my eye. He's looking at me, not inspecting me or judging me, just looking. His eyes are soft but not with pity; that's just how they are—warm and melting like hot butter. His eyes draw me in. They remind me of a forest, but not a dark, damp, depressing kind like I ended up in. His eyes are a forest where the sun always shines. They are the color of sap dripping down a tree with speckles of green from the leaves rustling in the breeze. I can almost hear it, the life of a forest, all in his eyes.

I realize I've probably been staring too long, so I disengage myself from the daydream of his eyes to see him smiling expectantly. I have already noticed, he has so many different variations of smiles, and you can truly tell the difference between each one. He's waiting for me to say something, and I am suddenly very embarrassed. I look down and ask, "Sorry, did you ask me something else?"

"Not exactly," he replies, no trace of annoyance or teasing in his voice. "I just said I don't think the Hannah you mentioned was the real Hannah. I want to know about you."

I chew on that statement for a second before reaching into the past for the pieces of myself that I abandoned in order to be the person I thought Julien would want.

"I was a Mommy's girl for sure. Maybe that's to be expected since my dad left when I was about five, but I considered my mom to be one of my best friends for the longest time. She worked really hard for long hours since she opened her own business, but we made sure to have mother/daughter time every night. She would teach me recipes, and, although it may have been a precursor to her wanting me to take over the bakery when she couldn't run it anymore, I loved cooking and baking with her. My other best friend—" Again, Bobbi's name lodges in my throat. I push the other words around her name, "We were really into horror and true crime – ironic, I guess. I even thought about being a coroner or forensic scientist. I loved that my last name was King, because I could pretend that I was related to Stephen King. I would even pretend he was my dad sometimes.

"I was Hannah Boyle for the first five years of my life. When Dad left, it didn't take Mom long to want us to be Kings again, and Dad didn't put up any sort of fight for me to stay a Boyle. Those were happy years, when I was close with my mom and ... my old friend. But I got restless. I was antsy to see the world and just have something more than I had. So, I threw it all away to be the person that would get the most attention. I got Julien's attention and was absorbed into the popular girl bubble. Jules and I traveled a little to surrounding states during the summers. I always felt good when we were traveling, but, once we came back here, it never felt like enough. I wanted the whole world all at once."

I fall silent. Art keeps quiet for a few moments as well, like he knows giving him so much information about myself would drain me. Then he asks, "Why won't you say your friend's name?"

I shut my eyes and try to swallow her name. "Like I said, I threw it all away."

"For a life that's no longer yours," Art answers cautiously. "You don't have to continue isolating yourself. You can go back to them now."

I let out a shaky breath I didn't realize I was holding in. "I don't think I'm ready yet."

"You will be seeing them, Hannah. At the funeral," he adds.

"I know," I sigh. "That's why I just wanted to stay here until then."

"Okay," he replies and squeezes my hand briefly.

Sitting and waiting was my plan but then I feel a strong tug in my gut. I get to my feet and put a hand on my stomach.

"Something wrong?" Art asks.

I remember he told me about this feeling. "That thing you mentioned before, when you felt like you were on a hook being reeled in. It's happening." I look to him, my apprehension likely obvious in my eyes. "What do I do?"

He stands in front of me and puts his hands on my shoulders. "It's alright, just relax. Close your eyes and take some deep breaths. When you open them again, you'll be where you need to be."

"Will you be there too?" I ask. The desperation I hear in my voice, like a child begging their mom not to leave before they fall asleep, embarrasses me. I look down and add, "I just don't know if I can do any of this on my own."

"I'll be there, Hannah," he answers and reassures me with a smile when I bring my eyes back to his. "All I have to do is picture you in my head and think about going where ever you go. I'll be right behind you."

He takes a small step back and nods his head at me in encouragement. I do as he said, closing my eyes and taking deep breaths. I don't feel anything, so I crack one eye open to see if Art is still there to ask if there was anything else I needed to do. From that quick peek, I can tell I'm no longer in the morgue, and my eyes shoot open.

I'm in an interrogation room. A single bulb above the table is the only source of light. One investigator sits at the table shuffling his papers and methodically laying them out while the other paces behind him. The second one looks to be in his late twenties or early thirties and is obviously wound up. The first one seems likely to be the other's superior. He's older, possibly in his fifties, and wholly collected. Julien sits at the other side of the table.

Frustration laces my voice as I ask aloud, "Why do they have him here?"

Art's voice behind me startles me. "Who is this?"

As he comes to stand by my side, I answer, "That's Julien, he's my ... was my boyfriend."

"Boyfriends and husbands are usually prime suspects," he points out.

"Look at his face!" I exclaim. Julien's nose and cheeks are still swollen, puffy, and bruised from the fight. I also notice a brace on his ankle. "How could they possibly think he could have been involved?"

"Maybe they think you fought back hard," Art shrugs.

"Well, they're wasting their time!" I huff.

The seated investigator finishes shuffling through his papers and looks up at Julien. "We really appreciate you coming in for us, Mr. Stoll. We would just like to take down your statement." He places a tape recorder on the table and presses record. "This is Detective John Winslow accompanied by Detective Dennis Radford speaking to Mr. Julien Stoll in regards to the case of Hannah King. The date is November fifteenth, time is 6:45 PM. Mr. Stoll, would you please state your name for me and begin your statement?"

"An officer took my statement before they carted me off to the hospital. Why are you wasting time interrogating me when that asshole is still out there?" Julien asks through clenched teeth. I wince at his voice, raw from all the screaming he did and breaking with emotion.

"Please, Mr. Stoll, this isn't an interrogation. We were put on the case and want to go over all the details personally. We need to hear your account with our own ears and corroborate it to your original statement," Detective Winslow says.

"You think you're going to catch me in some elaborate lie? You think I did this to my own face? You think I smashed my head against something to give myself a concussion and then hog-tied myself in the bedroom just so I could nearly break my ankle trying to get to my phone in the living room? Man do I feel relieved now, knowing they put the brightest bulbs on this case!" Julien's voice gets louder until he's screaming the last sentence, only making his voice break more. I worry he hasn't stopped screaming since that night.

The younger investigator, Dennis, stops his pacing. He slams into the table and turns off the recorder. He leans across to get his face as close to Julien's as he can. I have the feeling he's staying on his side of the table to deter himself from finishing what Dale started. "Listen to me, you dipshit," Dennis says. "I'm the one who found that poor girl's body out in those woods. I'm the first one who saw what this monster did to her. You don't know a damn thing about it! You want me to give you a detailed description of her broken, caved in skull?" Julien's face turns pale. Rage is boiling inside of me, made worse by the fact I know there's nothing I can do to stop Dennis's verbal assault. I turn to glare at him, but my rage melts away when I notice a tear sliding down his face.

"I can tell you every detail because I see her lying there in the snow every time I close my eyes. I couldn't even be a decent man and cover her up because I knew forensics needed her exactly as she was found in order to do a thorough examination. You think I'm not gonna bust my ass to find this guy?" Detective Winslow places the back of his hand against Dennis's chest. Dennis immediately backs away from the table but takes one final jab at Julien. "Drop the macho man bullshit and do what we fucking ask."

Detective Winslow's finger hovers over the record button. Before continuing, he turns to glare at Dennis and warns, "Don't do that again." Dennis nods and turns away. He places his fists against the wall and takes some deep breaths. Winslow focuses back on Julien and presses record. "Please, state your name and begin your statement."

"My name is Julien Stoll. Hannah is ... was my ... Hannah was with me the night of the attack."

"I'm sorry," Winslow interrupts. "Could you please state the date of the attack? And a possible timeline of events if possible."

Julien huffs and rubs his hands over his face out of habit. He flinches from the pressure on his injured nose. "It was November thirteenth in the evening. If it's a slow night at the bar, she usually gets off around 7:00 PM so it was probably around 7:10 when she got home. We immediately started fighting."

"Over what?" Dennis interrupts.

Julien glares at him, but looks back to Winslow to answer. "I lost my job. She wasn't happy about it, threw my Xbox controller at the wall. She had a temper." A ghost of the smirk I fell for tugs at his lip but quickly dissipates.

I go to him and try to place my hand over his, but my fingers pass right through him. I feel a pang in my chest and settle on kneeling beside him to get a better look at his face as he continues.

"She stormed off to take a shower, but we started fighting again when she came out which would probably have been around 7:30. She said the back door was open and blamed me, so we were arguing about that. We both said some pretty nasty things to each other during fights, and this one was no different. I don't know if I'll ever be able to forgive myself for that." He quickly brushes away a tear before it could fall. "Suddenly she wasn't yelling at me. She was yelling for me to watch out. I started to turn around, but the bottle came down before I could process any details. All I could tell was he seemed about my height but heftier. When I came to, I heard them in the bedroom so I charged in there. We wrestled on the floor, and I landed some solid punches to his ribs and stomach. Dude may have a broken rib."

"Tough guy," Dennis grumbles.

Julien's jaw clenches, but he doesn't turn to glare at Dennis. He continues, "The guy tied me up and threw me on the floor by the side of the bed. I could see Hannah tied to the bed staring at me, completely useless ... so I started fighting against the restraints, trying to loosen them. He was speaking real low to her. I couldn't hear anything he said, but Hannah looked shocked and scared. Then he got off the bed and came towards me. Hannah was begging him not to hurt me. I did hear him say 'I won't because I know you would never forgive me.' I don't know whether she realized who it was or not, but I think he certainly knew her and felt like he had some sort of connection to her."

I feel a surge of guilt for how I treated Julien that night. I basically told him he was cripplingly stupid, and yet here he was, getting so close to the truth. If I had only trusted him more and told him about Dale, he likely would have made the connection that very night. If I had only been my true self with him, not some vapid husk of a woman I believed attracted him, maybe then I would have seen and appreciated his complexities. If I had only ....

I reach up to trace his jawline like I used to do when he held me in his arms. No muscle in his body reacts to my touch. My fingers pass through his face effortlessly, and that suddenly seems very fitting. It's clear to me now that we never truly knew each other. There had always been a barrier between us, put there by me, that kept us from truly reaching each other, and there would be no reconciling that now. My hand drops back down to my side. I stand and back up to the wall catty-cornered to where Art stands silently. I can't look at him.

After Winslow finishes jotting down some notes, he urges Julien on by asking, "And that was when he kicked you in the head, correct?"

"Yeah, he said they needed a head start. When I came to, I maneuvered into a standing position by supporting myself against the wall. I tried hopping all the way to the living room. I made it past the kitchen counter before I rolled my ankle and toppled over. I inched across the floor the rest of the way and was able to get into a kneeling position over my phone. I used Siri to call 911. Pretty sure the time on my phone was 8:40-something."

Winslow nods as he jots down a few more notes before collecting all his papers back into his suitcase. Julien stands when Winslow does and takes his hand when he extends it. "Thank you very much Mr. Stoll for your time. My stenographer will type up a report from this recording which we will get you to sign. Other than that, if you think of anything else, no matter how small the detail may seem, give me a call. These are direct lines to me; I have my office phone and cell number on here."

He holds out a business card which Julien takes and places carefully in his wallet. Winslow still holds the tape recorder, which he motions for Dennis to take.

"Dennis, take this to Stella for me, will you?" he asks. He receives a grunt in reply, and Dennis glares at Julien as he passes before leaving the room. "I wanted to apologize for Detective Radford's outburst. He's been with us a few years now, but he's still considered a new recruit compared to some of the other guys. We haven't seen a case like this in at least a decade. None of us were prepared for it, especially not him. Being the one that found her, it's been very hard on him. I promise you though, I will get him taken off this case if I believe he has become unfit to continue, but I truly believe the boy has potential. I hope you can forgive him."

Julien shuffles his feet and shrugs. "Sure, it's all good," he mumbles.

Winslow gives him a thankful smile then holds out his hand again. "You're free to go. Remember, call me if you think of anything else. At any time, I mean that."

Julien shakes his hand again, thanks him, and walks away. Winslow leaves a moment after, heading in the same direction Dennis went. The door shuts, leaving me alone with my thoughts and my guilt—and Art, who approaches me gingerly. He leans against the wall beside me, not looking at me or saying a word, not rushing me. Just waiting.

"I want to walk back to the morgue," I finally say. I push off the wall and walk through the closed door.

"Are you sure there's nowhere else you'd rather stay?" Art asks as he follows me down the hall.

"I just don't think I'm ready to see anyone else tonight," I answer.

He doesn't say anything until we are back in front of the morgue. As we approach the entrance, he stops and starts rubbing the back of his neck. He looks like he has something to say, so I ask.

"There's just somewhere I want to go. Someone I want to check on," he answers. His hand drops back to his side. He gives me a forced casual smile. "But I'll be back soon!"

"Wait," I say, panic rising. "Can I come with you?"

"I don't know, Hannah. It's not an enjoyable place. It's incredibly depressing if I'm being completely honest. I don't think that's what you need to be around right now."

I gesture to the morgue. "You think this is Disney World or something?"

Art sighs and his hand goes to the back of his neck again. "Of course not, but—"

"Please, Art. I don't want to be alone."

His face softens, and he nods at me. "Alright, just do what I said before we went to the police station. All you've got to do is think about me and you'll follow."

"Do you think if we were in contact with each other I'd just be transported with you?"

Curiosity passes over his face, and he replies, "I don't know. I never really had anyone around to test any theories about this place."

"Well, let's give it a shot. If it doesn't work, I can just try to do it the way you said and hope I do it right."

"Alright, why not?" Art holds out his arm for me like the men in those period piece movies. "Are you ready, Madam?" he asks in a botched British accent.

I'm a bit shocked to find amusement lifting the corners of my mouth into a grin. I wrap my arm around his and close my eyes.

When I open my eyes we are in a hospital room. Art immediately untangles his arm from mine and goes to sit beside the small figure almost entirely hidden under blankets and stuffed animals in the bed. I want to give him some privacy, so I go to the window and look out at the trees surrounding the hospital and their vibrant fall leaves in the dying light of day.

Art was speaking softly to the child in the bed. When the room goes quiet, I make my way over to them. "Are we at St. Jude's?" I ask.

Art nods as he continues looking at the slight boy, concern etched deep in his face. "He wasn't doing so well when I left, but this is too sudden."

"Were you close? Is he family?" I ask tentatively.

"He's never seen me. He showed up after my time here. I stayed though, after I passed. For the kids and, of course, because I was never shown the light."

"Do you think that's really how it is to pass over? Seeing a light?" I ask. I was always curious about the workings of passing over and the afterlife. When I found myself floating down that dark river, I thought I had found the answer. But my light was just the lamp in the morgue.

"I've seen some of these kids pass over. I never see the light, but they do," Art replies.

I'm about to ask him how he knows they saw a light, but the kid startles both of us by asking in a thin voice, "Who are you?"

"Well buddy, you can call me Art," Art answers in a friendly voice, but when he turns to me, I see panic in his eyes. "This is my friend Hannah."

"Do you know where my mom went?" the kid asks as he scans the room under heavy eyelids.

"She'll be back soon," Art says. "She loves you more than a ton, you know that? Does she tell you how proud she is of you?" The boy nods and attempts a smile. "That's because you are doing such an amazing job. You're a fighter, kid. I know you're tired, but the fight is worth it, hear me?" The boy's eyes clear and focus more on Art as he speaks. He nods solemnly at Art's last question.

Two women enter the room. One is a nurse who begins cheerfully engaging the kid in small talk as she bustles around him. She gives him a shot of something before heading out to try cheer up another sick child. The other woman is the kid's mother who sits beside him and immediately begins petting his hair and peppering his forehead with kisses.

When the nurse leaves, the boy looks off to his side where Art and I are standing. He looks confused and turns to his mom. "Where did Art and Hannah go?" he asks.

"Who's that, baby?" his mother asks.

"They were in here when you came back. Didn't you see them?"

A look of confusion mixed with fear shadows the mother's face before she hides it for her child's sake. "No baby, I didn't see anyone," she says, trying to sound nonchalant.

"They were nice. Art told me I'm a fighter. He told me I'm amazing."

The mother's eyes become glassy with tears, but the smile she beams at her son is as warm as the sun. "He was right, baby. You're the strongest boy ever."

I look to Art who is smiling at the scene in front of us. No trace of panic is left on his face. He turns to me and says, "Let's go back now."

I nod, and he wraps an arm around my shoulder. We close our eyes on the hospital and open them back in the morgue.

"How could he see us, Art?" I ask.

"People can see us ... if they are getting close to the end."

"You mean that kid was—" I can't finish my question.

"I never saw someone bounce back so quick like that. I mean some of the kids who ended up seeing me did get better, but it took time. I can't imagine a single shot from the nurse would have made him that much better so quickly. So maybe—"

I wait a few seconds, watching Art's crinkled face, before I get too curious and ask, "Maybe what? What are you thinking?"

"Well, I couldn't say for sure, but maybe he was thinking about giving up. Maybe he wanted to stop fighting," Art replies. He rubs his hands over his face and shakes his head sadly.

"If that was the case," I say, sitting down next to him and squeezing his shoulder. "Then you saved him."

Art gives me a weak smile and says, "No matter what the cause was I just hope he continues trying. I hope he beats it."

"Me too," I agree. After a few more seconds I say, "If your theory is right though, that would mean that anyone who's truly ready to give up on life would be able to see us too?"

Art sits a bit straighter, looks at me, and shrugs his shoulder. "It's a possibility," he says before letting out a huff of breath and continuing, "I wish I had some clear answers for you. I feel like I haven't learned a single thing these two years, and I popped in here saying I can help you." He shakes his head at himself and tries to apologize, but I cut him off.

"You stayed at that hospital for two years?" I ask. He doesn't reply so I ask, "Why?"

"I guess I didn't know where else to go."

"Bullshit," I immediately reply. I hold my breath, cursing the fact I have no filter, but Art chuckles.

"Yeah, that's valid," he sighs. I wait quietly to see if he will give me a real answer or if I should change the subject. He continues, "I thought it was where I needed to be. I thought my life's purpose was to end up there and die there so I could then be like a guide to these confused kids on how to pass over. It became clear that I was off base with that considering I didn't know a single thing that could help them. They all saw their light and I was just there to watch them go—maybe give a little encouragement here and there. Most of them wanted to go into whatever it was they saw. I mean no hesitation. Some wanted to bring me, but I couldn't follow them. I tried, and I ended up just walking through the wall into the next room over."

"You thought you needed to spend eternity watching children die, and you were okay with that?" I ask, sadly. "Art, if that were true, this would be such a cruel universe."

He looks deep into my eyes and asks, "Like it hasn't already shown itself to be exactly that?"

I could agree with that sentiment considering what my fate turned out to be, but I want him to go back to his obnoxiously optimistic, cheerful disposition so I ignore him. "There could be any number of reasons we didn't pass on. Maybe there was a glitch, and we're stuck here by no fault of our own. We could have unbalanced karma that needs to be evened out. We could also have unfinished business—like me and Dale, or maybe I need to somehow make amends with the people I hurt. Can't you think of anything? Anyone you left on bad terms?"

"I can't go there, Hannah."

"Not even after two years? Not even if it means you can move on?"

"Hannah, please."

I see the pain in his eyes and pump my brakes. It comes to me suddenly that staying at the hospital was a distraction for him, and I'm the same. I vow to myself I won't move on and leave him behind. I'll make him face whatever he's scared to face. But not yet. Right now, I just want to make the storm clouds in his eyes dissipate.

"Okay, Art. If we are in this together though, that means we help each other, understand? I won't leave you behind." He studies my face for a moment and searches my eyes for the truth in my words. He must see it because he gives me a genuine smile.

"Thank God," I blurt out. In response to his confused look, I say, "Doom and gloom don't really fit you. Peppy and cheerful are more your style."

His smile widens. "You think I'm peppy?" he chuckles.

I smile back and roll my eyes. "Excessively peppy," I tease. "I've gotten used to it though. It's sort of refreshing. And without it you are nearly unrecognizable."

We laugh, then sit quietly for a moment before he puts his hand over mine and squeezes it.

"Thank you," he says, and my non-beating heart skips a beat.

We spend the rest of the night talking. I tell him more about my mom, and he tells me more about his siblings and their families. We avoid unpleasant topics; he doesn't ask about Dale and I don't ask about his mother. It's clear to me that she was the sore topic in his life as the only thing he ever said about her was that her mother was from Columbia. I don't want to push him right now but keep that revelation in the back of my mind to revisit later. I also tell him about Bobbi and some stories from when we were close. He doesn't ask what happened between us, and I don't offer those details. Yet.

Our conversation ends when the morgue workers remove my body from storage in preparation for the funeral home.

"The family didn't want to try reconstruction?" asks one of the workers as they move my enshrouded body onto a metal cart.

"The mom seemed interested when we brought it up, but the dad shot it down. He said they should do the funeral quick so the grieving process isn't drawn out," the other answers. The last sentence was ladened with disgust. Clearly my father has made his usual impression. "I could tell the mom wanted to talk about it more, but the poor woman didn't look like she had the fight in her."

"Makes sense. Wasn't she the one who had to identify the body?"

"Yeah, the dad showed up with her the next day to talk about what arrangements needed to be made but declined to see his daughter." The word declined was drawn out and dripped venom.

"Fucking prick," the other worker agrees as they roll my body away to an awaiting hearse.

I feel Art's hand rest on my shoulder making me twitch slightly. "Are you alright, Hannah?" he asks.

"I'm fine," I answer through gritted teeth. "Not like it comes as any surprise to me that my father just wants to get this over with as quickly as he can so he can go back to his perfectly manicured life with his new, botoxed, doll of a wife."

"Hannah," Art repeats and reaches down for my hand, which I unconsciously have clenched into a tight fist.

I sigh and force every muscle in my body to relax. "I'm fine," I say again. Art doesn't look convinced, so I'm about to reassure him when I feel a tug in my gut. My hand immediately goes to my stomach. I look at Art and tell him, "It's happening again."

He doesn't need any explanation. He replies, "Lead the way."

W e find ourselves in a meeting room with the familiar faces of Detectives John Winslow and Dennis Radford seated on one side of a foldable table. Detective Winslow is going about his routine of setting up his notebook, papers, and tape recorder just how he likes them. Dennis is pacing around the room as usual. I turn from them to look out the windows and verify we are at the college.

The speaker in the room and every speaker around campus crackle before the voice of the dean scratches its way out. "Good morning students. As I'm sure you all know, later this evening will be the wake and funeral of fellow student, Hannah King. Keep her and her dear family in your thoughts and prayers today, and I encourage you to attend the ceremony this evening at Redbrick Memorial at 6:00 to give her family your condolences. In the wake of such a tragic loss of one of our own, I have promised the dedicated officers working on this case that we will all be of assistance to them on this most somber of days. When you hear your name over the speakers, or if you have any information which you deem pertinent to the case, make your way to meeting room one on the third floor. We will begin by asking Christine Meyers and Shelley Stevens to please make your way to meeting room one. Thank you all for your cooperation, and remember to stay strong during this distressing time."

"Oh God," I groan.

"What?" Art asks. "I thought it was sincere."

"Not the dean," I correct him. "Christine and Shelley. No hiding who I was from you now," I mutter to myself.

"Hey," he places a hand on my shoulder and holds eye contact. "Who we hang out with doesn't define who we are."

I look away. "No, but our actions do. I did horrible things in order to fit in with them, and those things are all on me." I shrug away from him and sit on the table beside Winslow.

When the elevator clunks up to the third floor, I can immediately hear Christine and Shelley chittering to each other as they walk down the hall. Their giggling escalates just outside the door before they compose themselves and enter the room somberly together. I find myself sympathizing with Dennis as he has to contain the urge to groan and roll his eyes.

Winslow, ever the diplomat, smiles warmly at them and says, "Good morning, ladies. We would actually like to speak to each of you privately. If one of you would care to wait out in the hall? We put out a few chairs outside that door there."

"Of course, sir," Shelley answers obediently in her best innocent schoolgirl voice, the one she uses when she is trying to seduce older men. I tilt my head back and groan loud enough for me and Dennis both. "I'll wait for you right out here," she says smiling shyly, tilting her head down to look at him from under her eyelashes. She bats them at him and hugs the door frame for a second before turning the corner, trying her best to stick her skinny butt out so it is the last thing he sees of her.

Dennis shuts the door behind her and takes his place beside Winslow, who is either oblivious or unfazed by the Shelley fiasco. He starts off the same way he did during the interview with Jules – stating the two detectives' names; the date, time, and place of the interview; and asking Christine to state her full name and to classify how she "knew the victim."

"My name is Christine Meyers," she states cheerily, clearly loving the drama and attention. "Me, Hannah, and Shelley are just the best of friends. I mean, we're practically sisters. Or, I suppose I should say, were. It is such a tragedy." She snatches a tissue from her purse and dabs her eyes.

"Yes it truly is, and I am so sorry for your loss," Winslow consoles. She gives him her sweetest smile. When he looks down to his notebook, she steals a glance at Dennis and bites her lip. She waves at him coyly before focusing back to Winslow as he asks, "How did you meet Hannah? How long have you been friends?"

"It's been about four years," Christine answers. "We met pretty soon after she started dating Jules. We didn't hang around the same people before then, but from the moment me and Shelley first met Hannah, we clicked and just knew we'd be forever friends," she finishes, choking herself up on those last two words and dabbing her eyes again.

"When was the last time you saw her?" Dennis asks.

Christine is more than happy to turn her attention to Dennis. "That very same night," she breathes out, bottom lip trembling. "We went to see her at work."

"Was anything different about Hannah that evening? Or did you notice anyone strange at the bar?" Dennis asks.

"No Sir, not that I can recall. We were just—" Christine pauses and puts her finger to her lips. "You know what?" she asks no one, then pauses for dramatic effect. Dennis's pen tapping against the table marks the seconds. "We did have a bit of a run in with Bobbi and Mark," Christine says.

I want to scream in her face and tear her hair out by the roots. Did she seriously not remember the creepy man staring at me at the end of the bar? I get up from the table and storm over to the trash can by the door which I attempt to kick to the other side of the room, but my foot just goes straight through it. I grit my teeth and lean against the wall.

"Do you know their last names, by any chance?" Winslow asks.

"I think they're Bobbi Willow and Mark Hammer? You should ask Shelley though. She's way better with names."

Winslow nods to Dennis, and he's on his feet. He peeks out into the hallway and asks Shelley about Bobbi and Mark's last names. "Bobbi Willow and Mark Tanner," Shelley answers, genuinely happy to be of use. She hears Christine laugh so she peeks around the corner into the room. "What are you laughing at?"

"I said his last name was Hammer," Christine admits and laughs again.

Shelley rolls her eyes at Winslow and giggles. "She really is helpless."

Winslow smiles patiently back at her then gives Dennis a particular look.

"Thank you for the clarification. We'll be with you in just a minute. We just have one more question for your friend." Dennis says.

"Okay, sure," Shelley says. She tries to catch Winslow's eyes one more time, but the door shuts in her face.

Dennis gets on his walkie-talkie and asks for Bobbi Willow and Mark Tanner to be called to the meeting room in five minutes. He then sits back down next to Winslow, who continues his questioning. "What happened with Bobbi and Mark that evening?"

"Well, you see, Bobbi and Hannah used to be friends back in like middle school. Hannah has been trying to shake her for years, but Bobbi is like totally obsessed with her. So, Bobbi shows up, and I'm all like, oh my god. So, I tried to go intercept but I guess I had a few too many to drink. I sort of tripped on my own feet and my drink just spilled all over Bobbi. Mark was totally furious. His face was stoplight-level red."

Winslow nods as he finishes up his notes then looks back up for one final question. "Ms. Meyers, can you think of anyone that would have wanted to hurt Hannah?"

Christine opens her mouth but nothing comes out. She bites her lip and sits silently for a moment before answering, "Look, Hannah could be a bitch but I don't think anything she did would drive someone to murder her."

Dennis's head snaps in Christine's direction. "This is your dead best friend you're talking about and you call her a bitch?"

Christine flinches but composes herself quickly. She always disguised fear with anger, so she turns her fiery eyes on Dennis and snaps, "I've known her for four years, Detective," the last word drenched in sarcasm. "How long have you known her?"

Dennis clenches his jaw but controls his temper under Winslow's gaze. "Thank you, Ms. Meyers. You're free to go back to class. Please tell your friend to come in."

Christine nods to Winslow and makes sure not to look in Dennis's direction. She flips her hair at him before turning her back and walking out the door. I hear her tell Shelley it's her turn and that she'll wait in the hall for her.

Shelley goes through the same set of questions, most of her answers being the same as Christine's. Shelley gives a more accurate depiction of what happened between Mark, Bobbi, and the three of us, but she also does not mention the man at the end of the bar.

"Bobbi went up to the bar and grabbed Hannah's hand. She looked super uncomfortable, so Christine went and dumped her drink all over Bobbi. Her shirt was soaked through and um..." She pauses, peeking with fake embarrassment at Winslow.

"Please, we need any details you can provide. We need an accurate picture of what occurred on that night," he encourages her.

Shelley nods obediently and takes a deep breath before continuing, "Well, her shirt was white so we could all see that she wasn't wearing a bra. Poor Mark was so embarrassed. See, his religion forbids premarital sex. He and Bobbi never ... you know."

"And how would you know a fact like that about their personal lives? If you weren't friends?" Dennis asks.

"Well, I guess we don't know for certain, but Hannah teased them about it relentlessly," Shelley answers. She then tells them about the conflict earlier in the day when I'd picked at Bobbi for how short her skirt was. "Mark wasn't embarrassed that time. He was fuming. I could practically see smoke coming out of his ears. He told Hannah she disgusted him and that prayers wouldn't save her."

I peek at Art, who has been silent during both interviews, taking in every detail. I can't see any indication on his face of what he thinks about the things I did and said that day. He must feel me looking because he turns towards me.

I look away before our eyes meet.

Winslow jots down a few things then asks, "Did Hannah pick on a lot of people or just Bobbi and Mark?"

Shelley shifts into a more defensive mood. "Hannah wasn't a bad person, sir. Everyone has a mean streak. Look at Mark. He could have turned the other cheek. In fact, isn't that part of his religion? But he said hurtful things too. It's just in our nature. Nothing Hannah ever said to anyone should have caused this. She didn't deserve it."

I soften to Shelley then. I always liked her a bit more anyway. She seems more genuine and caring than Christine. There were moments in our friendship, always when we were away from Christine, where I almost told her things I had only ever told Bobbi. Like how I always felt empty, like something vital was missing in me. Or about Dale.

"No," Winslow agrees, "I would never imply Hannah, or anyone for that matter, deserves to end in such a fashion. I'm deeply sorry if that's what my words seemed to suggest." Winslow places his hand over Shelley's, which causes her to brighten.

"I'm sorry," she replies with an embarrassed smile. "I've been getting really emotional at the most random things lately."

"That's to be expected, dear," he replies, and pats her hand before withdrawing. He hands her one of his business cards. "If you think of anything else, call me. Any time of the day or night. No matter how small the detail may seem."

Shelley holds it reverently in her hand as Dennis ushers her out and calls for Bobbi to come in.

As Winslow is putting a new tape in his recorder and rear-ranging his things, I listen to Christine, Shelley, and Mark on the other side of the door.

"It was so awkward out here," Christine whispers to Shelley. "I'm pretty sure Bobbi broke up with Mark."

"You know I'm sitting right here, right?" Mark asks. "I can hear you."

Ignoring him and what Christine just said, Shelley croons, "He gave me his number!"

Christine sighs and says, "Shelley, he gave me a card too. He's giving them to everyone so people will call with tips. You know, for the murder case?"

"Well, did he put his hand over yours?" Shelley asks.

"I don't want your old man detective, Shelley. The other one was way hotter, but he's an asshole," Christine says. I can hear the pout in her voice.

"You two are truly revolting," Mark says. "You do realize what we're here for right? You could have a little respect for the situation."

"You're too uptight, Mark," Christine replies. "No wonder Bobbi left you. It was only a matter of time. Girls have needs too."

"Plus, what respect did you ever show to Hannah?" Shelley hisses before she and Christine stomp away.

I'm glad to hear Winslow start his interview so I can focus on that and not think about how nothing I did in life merited respect from Mark, or anyone else for that matter.

Focusing on Bobbi's words isn't easy though. Seeing her and listening to her again makes memories, good and bad, crash through me like a tsunami. With the memories, a cacophony of emotions roll through me as well—nostalgia, comfort, joy, sadness, regret, and anger at myself.

"How long have you known Hannah? Tell me a bit about your relationship with her from when you met to the time of the crime," Winslow asks.

"We were friends since we were in diapers practically," Bobbi says with a smile on her face and tears brimming her eyes. "We lived next door to each other. Our moms became close very quickly, and we became best friends. Maybe it was simply because we spent most of our time together that made us have the same interests and connect so deeply, but it really felt like we were soulmates. I guess that sounds like a bit much coming from someone who hasn't really seen her or talked to her much in the last four years." Her words are like a wrench clamping down on my heart and twisting tightly.

"Hey, you don't need to worry about that in here, alright?" Dennis says. He speaks in the calmest voice I've heard from him. It makes perfect sense to me that Bobbi would bring out the caring side of this angry detective. She brings out the best in everyone. "We've spoken to Hannah's boyfriend and her two friends already, so we have an idea of what she was like for the past four years. We want to know more about her past, people from her past especially. The more we know about her the better."

"Have you talked to Hannah's mother? Did she mention Dale?" Bobbi asks.

"We haven't been able to speak to her extensively yet. Can you tell us more about Dale? Who is he in regards to Hannah?" Winslow asks. He seems more alert than he had been with Christine and Shelley.

"Dale lived across the street from Hannah. After Hannah's dad left, he became almost like a stepdad for her. I don't know if he and Ms. Carolyn actually dated, but he was around a lot. Things became ... inappropriate though. There was an incident, and Ms. Carolyn cut him out of their lives. He was at the bar the night Hannah was killed. I saw him staring at her."

Finally, his name was mentioned. I relax muscles I didn't know I'd clenched. All I can think is, *God bless you, Bobbi.* Even after shutting her out and teasing her afterwards, Bobbi still wants to help me however she can. I don't deserve it, but I'm so grateful for it—and for her. She's still one of the most important people in my life. I never really allowed anyone else to take her place.

Winslow is speedwriting, clearly glad for a possible lead. "Would you happen to know his full name?"

Bobbi thinks for a moment before shaking her head. "Ms. Carolyn would know. If you need the specifics of what happened between him and Hannah years ago, I think you should ask her too. I don't feel like that's something I should tell."

Winslow stops writing and looks Bobbi in the eyes. He says, "Ms. Willow, while I understand your hesitancy comes from a place of respect for Hannah's privacy, we need any details you can give us."

Bobbi looks down at the desk in silence for several moments before taking in a deep breath and saying, "Okay, I understand. I want to help as much as I can."

Winslow meets her gaze when she looks back up at him and says, "Thank you, Ms. Willow. I know this is a difficult time for you, but we greatly appreciate your help." He nods encouragingly for her to proceed.

Bobbi takes another steadying breath then begins, "Hannah told me before that when she was twelve, she ended up alone with Dale in the kitchen while everyone was out in the backyard having a barbeque. He came up behind her and, at first, just put his hands on her shoulders. She tried to brush him off, but then he wrapped his arms around her waist and held her tight against him. She said she could feel, you know, his crotch. He was rubbing against her. She said her struggling against him just made him more excited. Luckily, someone walked in so he let her go, and she ran right to her room and locked the door."

As Bobbi finishes, I look to Winslow and Dennis. Winslow nods and jots a couple of notes down on his notepad. His face seems stony as he tries to maintain his professionalism, but I notice the minute movement of his jaw clenching and the way he presses the pen harder into the pad than usual. Dennis, on the other hand, is much more transparent. His eyes can't hide his anger and disgust.

"And that incident is the last known time Dale and Hannah were together?" Winslow asks.

"It was definitely the last time Dale was ever at their house. I don't know if Ms. Carolyn went to the police or not, but he was never put in jail. I think they just tried their best to avoid him," Bobbi says.

"I see. Now, could you tell us what happened at the bar that night you saw Dale speaking to Hannah?" Winslow asks.

"Mark and I went there to have dinner. We were seated close to the door, so I noticed when Dale walked in. He saw Hannah and headed straight to the bar. After she took his order, she turned to walk away and he grabbed her arm. I couldn't hear what they were saying, but she looked really shaken up. I kept glancing over at the bar as we ate, and Dale was always staring at her. When he finally left, I went up to the bar to see if Hannah was okay. She tried to blow the whole thing off because Christine and Shelley were there. Then Christine spilled her drink all over me and Mark practically dragged me away."

Hearing Bobbi explain what happened and how concerned she was only makes me feel more guilty about how I treated her that night. She had been keeping a close eye on Dale, probably ready to step in at any moment. She had my back in a way not even Julien could have if he had been there. Throughout these last four years, Bobbi has stayed on the outskirts of my life but never truly walked out for good. She never closed that door, even though she had every reason to. She kept her hand extended no matter how many times I swatted it away.

If I had taken it that night, would things have turned out differ-ent? The weight of my thoughts drags my body down the wall until I sit slumped on the floor. After a couple of moments I feel Art sit beside me and gently pat my back. I can't face him, but I look back up when Winslow continues his questions.

"Can I ask why you worded it that way? That Mark 'dragged' you away?" he asks.

"Oh," Bobbi shrugs. "I guess I'm being a little dramatic. He was embarrassed because Shelley pointed out that I wasn't wearing a bra. Me and Mark... things between us always felt complicated and a bit off to me. We don't have the same views on most things. At first, his strong beliefs and the surety they brought him about himself was what drew me to him. Recently though, his self-righteous 'preaching'—which is frankly not far-off from plain old bullying—his controlling nature, and his insistence on pushing his beliefs onto me just got to be too much. I couldn't take it anymore. He told me I was 'a tramp, just like Hannah.' That was the last straw for me. He hated Hannah. It always bothered me, but it used to not be so venomous."

Dennis asks, "Why were you still so protective of Hannah, even after she constantly picked on you and your boyfriend?"

Bobbi answers as if the reason was too obvious to have even warranted asking, "Because I love her." The wrench clamped on my heart gives another hard tug. "Four years apart in the grand scheme of twenty-two years is nothing. That love doesn't go away. I could handle her teasing because I knew where it was coming from. Mark didn't."

"Could you explain it to us? Why you think Hannah teased you so much?" Winslow asks.

"The biggest difference between the two of us was that I was always thinking about the future while Hannah was only concerned with the here and now—what she could get now, the fun she could be having now, fleeting things in my opinion. That's what drew her to Julien. I don't know him personally, but he seems to be one of those people that does what they want, when they want. Plus, he's exciting—always riding around on his motorcycle and not afraid to get into a fight. She was sort of an adrenalin junkie. She saw him, wanted to have that sort of life, so she changed into the kind of person she assumed he would be into. That's where Christine and Shelley came in, and that's when the teasing started. She was just trying to fit in with them in order to keep this new life she made for herself."

It's almost eerie how spot on Bobbi's explanation is, but it doesn't really surprise me. Like she said, four years apart after so long together doesn't make all those memories and emotions go away. She was on my mind more than I would have ever admitted during these past four years, and I must have been on her mind as well.

Winslow nods thoughtfully then looks over his notes. His eyes catch on something. "Ms. Willow, you mentioned that Mr. Tanner disliked Hannah. You said that recently this hatred has become 'venomous.' I have to ask you. Do you think Mark would have—"

Bobbi cuts him off before he can finish the question. "Absolutely not. Mark may be sanctimonious to a fault, but he's not a killer. He believes in hell too strongly to risk eternal damnation. He dropped me off at home right after dinner but I'm sure if you asked his roommate, you would find out he was at his apartment the rest of the night. Besides, I know who killed Hannah. I know it was Dale." She chokes back a sob. Dennis hands her a tissue which she presses against her eyes. She lets her tears fall. I hear another faint utterance of "I just know it was him," before she wipes her eyes one more time and blows her nose.

Bobbi accepts Winslow's card after composing herself. Both detectives walk her to the door. Dennis stops with his hand on the door handle. He places his other hand on her shoulder and says, "You take it easy, okay miss? We'll see Hannah gets the justice she deserves."

Bobbi wipes at her eyes and nods.

"And we will have to ask you to stay silent about your suspicions of this Dale character," Winslow says, almost apologetic. "Especially to Hannah's mother. We don't want hysteria and, if he is the killer, we don't want him catching scent of us on his tail."

Bobbi bites her lip but nods. "If you mention Dale's name to Ms. Carolyn, she's going to come to the same conclusion as me. She may even already suspect it, though she may not have had the time or the energy to think about it too much."

"If she does, we will tell her the same thing we just told you. We don't want anyone running before we can thoroughly investigate all the details," Winslow states in his most professional tone of voice to show how serious he is, and possibly to show how dedicated he is to solving this case.

Bobbi nods again, thanks them, and leaves the room. She doesn't even glance at Mark as she passes, but his eyes follow her down the hall. He only looks away after Dennis tells him it's his turn.

Mark sits across from Winslow, but stares past him at the wall. I can tell from the granite-hard look on his face that this interview will be hard to listen to.

After going through his usual introductions, Winslow starts his questioning. "Tell us what your relationship was like with Hannah."

Mark lets out a dry, bitter laugh. "My relationship with her? She liked to torment me, and I dreaded the sight of her."

I flinch at the malice in his voice because I know I deserve it.

"Do you have any idea why she chose to pick on you and Ms. Willow?" Winslow asks.

"She just wanted to ruin our relationship, which she finally succeeded in doing," Mark answers.

"Blaming your problems on a dead girl. That's pretty convenient," Dennis says in a deadpan voice as he glares at Mark. He doesn't break eye contact when Mark turns to him incredulously. For the first time, I want to hug Dennis tight.

"Not all my problems," Mark tries to backpedal. "Just with me and Bobbi. I mean, we were doing just fine before Hannah started hounding us these past few months. I tried to make her see what Hannah was doing, but Bobbi was always delusional when it came to her."

"What do you mean by delusional?" Winslow asks.

"When we first met, Bobbi told me stories of her best friend. She sounded like a nice girl who really cared for Bobbi. I wanted to meet her. That's when she told me that Hannah found a new group to hang out with so they don't really speak anymore. I thought it was sad but something that does happen fairly often. People drift apart. But then Hannah started saying horrible things to us when she saw us together. She was so far from the person Bobbi told me about, but Bobbi held fast to her version of Hannah. No matter what she did or what she said, Bobbi said 'she's still Hannah, she's still my best friend.' As if Hannah gave a single shit about her anymore. After every encounter with Hannah, she would defend her. As if Hannah was just confused. She refused to accept the fact Hannah changed. She wasn't the person she was when she was friends with Bobbi. She still refuses to accept it."

"So, you were trying to convince Bobbi to give up on Hannah?" Winslow clarifies.

"I was trying to protect her. I was trying to make her see that she wasn't the same person before she did something so horrible it broke Bobbi forever," Mark answers.

"Protect her, huh?" Dennis grumbles. He pauses, eyes dark and locked on Mark. "You claim your relationship ending is all Hannah's fault. You don't think you calling Bobbi a tramp had anything to do with it?"

Mark flinches and lets out his breath in a rush. His hands pass over his face, and he takes a deep breath. When his hands fall to his lap, he wears a miserable expression on his face. "I was just angry. I went too far. I've apologized to her again and again."

"Well, sometimes 'sorry' won't fix a damn thing," Dennis states.

Mark huffs and rolls his eyes. "Yeah, thanks for the relationship advice. What does this have to do with anything? Why are we talking about my relationship problems?"

Winslow answers, "You were clearly very angry with Hannah. You blame her for your problems with your girlfriend."

Mark gapes at the detectives. "Are you implying that I did this?"

"Ms. Willow doesn't seem to think you did," Winslow assures him. "We'd like to hear from you about your whereabouts after leaving the restaurant."

An exasperated noise whines from Mark's open mouth. He throws up his hands then crosses his arms. "Fine," he says. "I dropped Bobbi off at home and went back to my apartment."

"Would you happen to remember what time you got home?" Winslow asks as he writes.

"I don't know," Mark answers. He's given up on trying to control the annoyance creeping into his voice. "Wouldn't have taken me more than 15 minutes to bring Bobbi back home and then get back to my apartment, so maybe sometime around 7:00 PM."

"Your roommate, was he home when you got there?" Winslow asks.

"Yeah, he was."

"Does he go to school here?"

Mark rolls his eyes and answers, "Yeah, his name is Austin Harris."

Winslow jots down the name then stands. Mark follows, clearly ready to be dismissed.

"Here is my card," Winslow hands it to Mark at the door. "Call me if you remember anything or come across anything you think may be important."

"Sure thing," Mark mumbles as he stuffs the card into his pocket and slinks out of the room.

I'm not all that interested in hearing from Mark's roommate, so I turn to Art and say, "Let's go down to the courtyard."

We walk through the school, then sit silently at one of the picnic tables. I let my mind race with everything that was said during those interviews. Christine and Shelley's nonchalance. Bobbi's despair. Mark's anger. It all burrows under my skin and crawls around in my veins until it pours into my heart. I've spent the past four years with people who hardly care I'm gone, leaving my one true friend crawling after me. I kept looking over my shoulder at her only to shoot her down time and time again. Why? To what purpose? Did I really want to hurt her so bad she wouldn't come back again, or did I want her to keep trying? I can't say anymore. I recall my disappointment in her when I first saw her with Mark, dressed like an innocent little church girl. Was it really disappointment, or was it jealousy because she smiled at him so warmly? I recall how I had to shake off her seeming indifference toward me in the courtyard that day I mocked Mark about his virginity. I told myself it was because it's more fun when I get a rise out of both of them. In reality, it stung when she disappeared inside the building without a single glance in my direction. Did I start to tease her because that's the only way I felt like I could keep her in my life?

I suddenly become aware of my fingers drumming against the table. I surface from my inner turmoil to ask Art, "Why do you think it is that I can sit at this table, drumming my fingers against it, but I can't kick a trash can over or touch anyone? I mean, there are stories about people getting scratched by ghosts and objects tossed around the room, right?"

Art scratches the back of his head and shrugs. "My theory is that doing things like sitting down or leaning against a wall are so mundane that it doesn't take any mental energy to accomplish. Kicking or tossing an object, or touching a living being, though, that takes more energy than we realize. Takes a lot more concentration. Those vengeful spirits, if they're real, must have an immense amount of violent energy stored up to make such an impact and cause all that chaos."

I sit thoughtfully for a few moments before saying, "Or they have enough determination to make it happen."

Art looks at me as if he were trying to solve a puzzle. For a moment, I think I see something flicker in his eyes. Something like curiosity. Or maybe hope.

Neither of us seem to know what to say next, but it's a comfortable silence so we continue to sit in it. Then a bell rings and people swarm into the courtyard around us. We jump up from the table to avoid people sitting on us—or in us.

I notice Art scowling at a group and see Christine and Shelley at the center of it. Their words come to me, and I roll my eyes.

"You guys should all come. This is definitely what Hannah would have wanted instead of a dreary wake. She loved parties! She would want us to have fun in her memory, not dress in black and go cry with a bunch of old people," Shelley says, projecting her voice so more people than those surrounding her might hear.

"Our Hannah remembrance party starts at 6:00 at my house," Christine calls out to the courtyard. "We only get two hours to properly say goodbye to Hannah because of the curfew. Me and Shelley were Hannah's best friends. We know she would want to be remembered with a night of drinks, laughter, and fun. Anyone who wants to come will be more than welcome. My house is your house!

See you then."

Christine and Shelley strut away together, leaving an excited murmur in their wake.

Art turns to me with the most incredulous look on his face. He notices my slightly amused expression and opens his mouth to say something but nothing comes out.

"Please," I say, rolling my eyes. "I knew there was no way in hell that Christine and Shelley would show up to a wake. And I don't know most of these people." I gesture to the flood of people passing around us, spreading the news of the party to others. "They can do what they want, what do I care?"

"It's still disrespectful," Art mutters.

"Don't be offended on my behalf," I say, then lower my eyes. "Did you not hear everything that was said during those interviews? It's not like I did much to garner any respect."

"Hey," Art says, forcefully but also with the ever-present gentleness in his voice. He takes my hand in both of his. It's such a caring gesture I look up at him in surprise. He locks his eyes on mine and continues, "We are not the things we have done in the past. It's what we do moving forward and how we make amends that truly matters."

"And what am I supposed to do now?" I ask. "What can I possibly do that could make a difference?"

He holds my gaze and says, "You can forgive yourself, Hannah."

I find myself wishing I could cry.

10

Art and I are the first ones to show up for the wake. We watch as several flower arrangements are carted in and arranged around my casket. They consist of delicate white flowers with lots of small petals fanning out and purple roses, which I've never seen before.

My parents are the next to show up. When I see my mom, my breath is knocked out of me. She's so pale the dark bags under her eyes are barely concealed under a thin layer of makeup. What she carries in her arms tugs hard at my heart-strings. She has a bundle of handmade papier-mâché tiger lilies, my favorite flower. She heads straight to the casket, passing the funeral home director without a glance. She places her arrangement on top and stares at it for a long moment. I don't think she would have moved if it wasn't for my dad impatiently pulling her back to the director, who's waiting to give his condolences and explain how the wake will proceed.

After the director leaves the room, an uncomfortable silence falls between my parents. A couple of minutes pass, then a slideshow starts playing of pictures my mom must have chosen. She watches it misty-eyed. My dad's attention is on his phone. Art also watches the procession of pictures with a soft smile.

I hear footsteps and turn to see my aunt walking down the aisle that splits the rows of pews. My mom turns as if in a dream, but her eyes clear when she sees her sister. She's unsteady on her feet as she rises.

Aunt Claire quickens her pace, heels clacking, and pulls my mom into a tight embrace. Tears begin to escape down my mom's cheeks.

"Oh, my sweetheart," Aunt Claire coos. "I wish I could have come sooner."

"It's alright. I know your kids need you." My mom's voice comes out hoarse.

Aunt Claire kneels before my mom as she sits back down on the pew. "Yes, well, Jerry managed to get time off to keep an eye on the kids. So, I'm all yours for the next three days. I will do whatever I can, Carol."

"It really shouldn't be your job to care for me, but I appreciate it," my mom says, fighting between her stubborn independence and her need for comfort.

"Hey," Aunt Claire protests, cupping my mom's face in her hands. "I may be younger, but this is what sisters are for. We promised Mom, remember? We'll always be there for each other."

My mother nods, no longer trusting her voice to produce anything more than a sob. I know that look on her face. She's straining to keep it in. Aunt Claire knows it too. She wipes a rogue tear that seeps from my mom's eye, and doesn't say anything else. Her arm wraps around my mom's shoulder as she settles down in the pew next to her. She glowers at my dad when she notices him at the other end of the pew, eyes still glued to his phone. She decides not to make a scene, though, and turns her attention to the slideshow.

Aunt Claire is able to draw my mom out enough to engage in some reminiscences. They share stories based off the pictures my mom chose. It's a confusing mix of nostalgia, heartache, tenderness, and sadness. Their memories bring phantom smiles to their faces that fade too quickly from bitter loss. It's painful to watch, knowing I can't comfort them in any way.

I try to distract myself by admiring the tiger lilies my mom constructed for me, but there's an ache in them too. I can't look at the exquisite attention to detail without thinking of her shut away in the house by herself surrounded by papier-mâché and piles of tear-sodden tissue paper.

Luckily people begin to pour in, giving me something else to turn my attention to. Great aunts and uncles, cousins, friends of my mom's, and other members of the community that I vaguely recognize as seeing in passing either on the street or at the restaurant. I'm surprised to see a few acquaintances from college show up, choosing to be here instead of the party at Christine's.

I watch them all pass by the casket, not sure what to do since it's a closed casket service. They pause for a few beats, maybe uttering a soft goodbye, then go to give my mother their condolences. I stay beside her and listen to them all, no longer paying attention to who's walking in because it's starting to get crowded. They are all mixing and mingling together, making their way to the front when they are ready.

A quiet mewling noise escapes my lips when I see Julien walk up to my mom. He's wearing the only suit he owns, the one he wore to prom our senior year of high school. It's grown short, but only slightly. You can hardly notice, really. It makes a sad smile creep onto my face nonetheless.

"Ms. Carolyn, I …" Julien trails off. He's keeping his head angled down and his eyes averted. Perhaps trying to hide his tears, or maybe he mistakenly feels guilty.

Mom isn't having it. She cups his chin in her hand and raises it so their eyes meet.

"I'm so sorry I couldn't protect her," he whispers and tears cloud his eyes.

She shakes her head. "You stop that," she reprimands. "You did what you could, Julien. I know you did."

A tear slides down his face which she wipes away with maternal softness, then she pulls him in and holds him as he cries quietly.

My heart aches for him. I know he must feel so small right now, being cradled as he allows himself this moment of vulnerability. This is something I know his mother never gave him. I hope he continues to share his grief with mine. Perhaps it will make it easier on both of them.

He composes himself and pulls away. His hands cup her arms just above the elbow, trying to turn the situation around to him comforting her.

"You come see me any time you need to talk," my mom tells him. "Don't be a stranger."

"Yes ma'am," he promises, then moves away to find a place to sit.

After a few more people pass by, giving a hasty "I'm sorry" and a terse hug, Bobbi and her mother stand in front of us. They hug my mom tight. Their condolences are much more sincere.

"Oh, Carol. I know there's nothing I could possibly say to make the pain go away. Just promise not to bear it all on your own. I'm always just a call away," Bobbi's mother says.

"Me too, Ms. Carolyn. If you need anything, just call us," Bobbi adds.

"You two are truly a blessing," my mom says with a brief smile. "I will. We'll see each other soon. Promise."

They smile, nod, and give her kisses on her cheeks before moving away.

I keep my eyes on them as they move down the aisle. Someone catches Bobbi's eye, and she motions for her mom to find a seat then continues walking towards the back of the room. I follow her line of sight and realize she is heading toward Julien. Curious, I follow her.

"Hi," Bobbi says. "Julien, right? I'm Bobbi. You probably don't know—"

"Bobbi," Julien repeats. "Yeah, Hannah mentioned you a few times."

Bobbi is clearly thrown off. "Sh-she did?"

"Yeah," Julien says and scoots over a tad so Bobbi has enough room to sit. "It was weird. When she mentioned you, it almost seemed like it was a reflex. Like it was so natural she couldn't help it. But then she would get sort of … nervous? I'd ask her to tell me more. What else you two used to do together. Why you drifted apart."

"Why were you interested?" Bobbi asks.

"She never talked about stuff from before we met. She'd get super defensive when I tried to learn more about her past. Plus, I was kinda hoping that if I got her talking about you then she'd realize you were a way better friend than those bitches she always hung around with." He looks at Bobbi sheepishly. "I kinda hate them, to be honest."

Bobbi lets out a breathy laugh but covers her mouth to stifle it. "Yeah, well, you aren't the only one," she says, humor laced in her voice and a smile on her face.

There is a beat of silence between them, then Julien says solemnly, "I should have tried harder. We were together four years. How could I have not tried harder?"

Bobbi puts her hand over his and squeezes. "When it comes to love, I think the past doesn't play as important a role as we think it does. You don't have to know every single thing about a person to love them or have a good relationship with them. That doesn't lessen what you two had. And you shouldn't blame yourself."

Julien smiles at her. It's a sad smile, but it's also a genuine one, which makes me smile too.

I turn around to head back down the aisle toward my mom and freeze. Dale is there, standing in front of her. My paralysis breaks, and I run. I'm repeating "No, no, no, no," under my breath like a mantra.

Tears are slowly rolling down his cheeks, and he's saying some bullshit about how it's such a tragedy. I don't really register what it is he's saying because I'm trying desperately to hit him, scratch him, pull him away from her, but my hands just keep going through him. Then, he puts his arms around her. And I lose it.

A guttural growl rises from somewhere deep inside me. I storm over to the vases of flowers by my coffin and scream at the top of my lungs as I smack one of them as hard as I can.

It flies through the air and smashes against the wall with a loud crack. Broken glass lay amongst the flowers in a spreading pool of water. The room has gone quiet and still.

My mom's deep intake of breath can be heard around the room. I look to her first. She doesn't look scared at all. A small smile is creeping onto her face.

I'm pleased to see Dale backing slowly away from my mom. He looks terrified.

Finally, I turn to Art. He stares back at me in complete shock. His eyebrows raise, and his mouth opens and closes. My mouth has fallen open in shock and confusion too. All I can do is shrug.

"Oh my God, it's my baby!" my mom exclaims. A manic look of excitement is plastered on her face. She goes to the pile of flowers and glass shards and looks around the room. "Hannah, where are you baby?" Receiving only baffled stares by everyone in the room, she gets down on her knees and puts her hand on the pile.

My dad finally breaks from his trance and hurries to her side.

"Carolyn, seriously, get a grip. Get off the floor and don't touch that. You're going to cut yourself."

He grabs her upper arm and tries to hoist her up, but she smacks his hand away and glares up at him. "Don't you dare tell me what to do or put your hands on me. This was a typical Hannah tantrum. She's here! I know it!"

He rolls his eyes and lets out an exasperated huff of breath. "Carolyn, stop it this instant. You know that's not possible. Hannah is in that box. She's gone!"

A look of unadulterated rage passes over my mom's face. She grabs one of the large glass shards and stands facing my dad. He sees the sharp object in her hand and takes several steps back.

"You're glad she's gone, aren't you? I never want to hear her name from your mouth ever again, you understand?" my mom says. She's pointing the shard steadily at my dad.

Suddenly, Detective Winslow is at her side. I didn't even realize the police officers were here but, sure enough, I look toward the aisle and see Dennis telling everyone to stay back.

"Ma'am, will you give me that glass shard? I don't want you to get hurt," Winslow says.

My mom looks to her hand and seems surprised at what she's holding. She lowers her hand and looks to Winslow. "I'm not crazy. Everyone saw. I know it was Hannah."

Winslow nods sympathetically. "We did see. Please, Ms. King."

My mom stares at his outstretched hand, confused. Then she remembers the shard and places it on his upturned palm.

My dad lets out a relieved sigh.

"Thank you," Winslow says to my mom and places a hand on her shoulder.

My mom doesn't seem to hear him or register his touch.

"I don't understand. It must have been one of her tantrums. But what made her so upset? I was just talking to—" her voice trails off. Her eyes drift up to look over Winslow's shoulder at Dale. Her mouth opens in shock, then rage flames up in her eyes.

Winslow notices and looks over his shoulder. He sees Dale and turns back to my mom. "Ms. King, would you come with me please?"

My mom is too overwhelmed to argue. She lets herself be escorted up the aisle and out the doors. I follow them with my eyes and catch a glimpse of Bobbi and Julien looking at each other, clearly shocked but curious too.

Dennis makes a "let's wrap this up" motion to the director who nods tersely and heads to the podium.

"We will now head to the cemetery. Once everyone is lined up in the funeral procession, we will leave together. God bless," he says into the microphone, then motions everyone to the door.

They all slowly trickle out, but I notice Dale stands paralyzed. He's staring at the carnage of flowers and glass. Confusion is etched into his face, but in his eyes there's only fear.

The burial is much less eventful, although I do notice my mom intermittently locking her eyes on Dale who stands nervously a few steps away from the crowd. He tries to act like he can't feel her eyes drilling into him, but he becomes more and more fidgety. His shaking fingers pick at the buttons on his jacket and tug at the sleeves. He brushes at his forehead often, either dealing with errant hairs or nervous sweat. He is the first to leave when the ceremony is over.

I watch as the crowd trickles out of the cemetery. Some give their last condolences to my mom, but many of them seem a lot more hesitant after her outburst in the funeral home.

Julien, Bobbi, and her mother are among the ones who stop to hug my mom one more time. Julien is first, promising again he won't be a stranger and would call her any time he needed to have a cry. He gives her a final hug before heading to the cemetery gate, where he stops and looks back as if waiting for someone.

Bobbi and her mom give my mom another bear hug. They are promising to get together one night soon when Bobbi notices Julien at the gate. He waves when her eyes fall on him, and she excuses herself with a final peck on the cheek for my mom.

Both women gaze at the pair. Bobbi's mom sighs and says, "I hope they can help each other through this."

My mom turns back to her friend and sighs in return. "Me too, Jean. They're good kids. They should stick together. I mean, I know it's been a while since the girls spent time together, but Hannah loved her."

"Bobbi knows, Carol," Jean says and cups my mom's hands in hers.

"Those girls Hannah hung around with didn't even have the decency to show up," my mom says.

"Would you have wanted them here anyway?" Jean asks.

"No, you're right," my mom says with a sigh. "Anything they'd have to say would have been fake. It just all makes me so angry, Jean. Every little thing makes me furious. It's all just so unfair."

Jean pulls my mom into another hug as sobs wrack her body, and all I can do is watch. I try to summon that strength or resolve, or whatever you want to call it, that let me smash the vase. I want so badly to hold her or at least brush a tear away from her cheek. I want her to feel me, to know how close I still am. No matter how hard I focus though, my fingers slip through her as easily as they pass through the air around me.

Bobbi comes running back and does what I can't. My mom passes from Ms. Jean's arms to Bobbi's. Before she fully envelopes my mother in her arms, Bobbi brushes away the tears rolling down my mom's cheeks as well as her own.

"I'm so glad you came for her, Bobbi," my mom sobs into Bobbi's shoulder. "Whatever happened between you two, I hope you know that she loved you."

"I do, Ms. Carolyn. I loved her just as much," Bobbi answers.

After another round of hugs and kisses, Bobbi and her mom go off together. My mom watches them go and looks to my aunt who is waiting outside the gate. She holds up a finger to indicate she'll just be a moment longer, and my aunt nods understandingly. My mom places her hand on my casket and looks around the cemetery.

"Hannah, I wish I knew where you were. Are you here?" my mom speaks to the air. "I just know it was you at the funeral home. Can you give me another sign? Anything at all?"

I do try. I try again to touch her. I try to shake the branches of a nearby tree with apples suspended amongst the leaves. It suddenly hits me, seeing nature continuing its unstoppable cycle, that I am truly stuck. How many seasons will I see come and go while I walk the earth unseen by everyone and everything going about their normal existences? My limbs feel very heavy all of a sudden. I think I may sink deep into the crust of the earth, too weighty to be supported by this steady planet any longer, incorporeal or not.

My mother's sigh brings me back to myself and my current surroundings. I return to her side, but I make no move to touch her. I don't have the energy to disillusion myself again.

"Were you trying to tell me it was him? Was it Dale?" she asks. Her fingers cease caressing the casket and ball into a fist. "Of course, it was. Who else could it have been? It's so obvious. I swear to you, Hannah, I will do whatever it takes to see him punished for what he's done. No matter how long it takes, I'll never give up. If the police do, I'll just kill him myself."

The surety and resolve in her voice worry me, especially at her murderous intent. If I were to be alive and she threatened to kill someone who upset me, we would have laughed it off and buried my sorrows in sweets. This time, I know, without a shadow of a doubt, that she means every word. I send out a prayer to a god I never fully believed in—and, if actually real, I'm not a hundred percent certain hasn't completely abandoned me—to please let the case close in a timely manner so my mother doesn't end up in jail for life.

"Did you see the tiger lilies I made you?" my mom asks, switching from homicidal to motherly in the blink of an eye. "They told me that they would put them in there with you. I hope you like them. I hope they bring you some comfort. I love you so much, baby. You will always be in my heart. If you are hanging around because of me, you don't need to worry. I want you to be at peace, not fretting over me. If it's because of Dale, well, Mama will make sure to fix that. He will pay for what he did to my baby. I'll do anything for you, sweetheart. I love you."

I watch her walk away with a feeling of foreboding. I feel like I have whiplash from all the sudden shifting from mourning to murderous. It's clear she has a tenuous grip on her sanity, but it's not like I can blame her for it. Like they always say, people process grief and trauma in different ways. You can never guess how you or anyone you know will react until it happens. Anger happens to be what my mother landed on, and what mother wouldn't when faced with the brutal murder of her only child? I can only hope and pray that nothing life-ruining comes from that anger.

I start to follow after her and quicken my pace when I see Detective Winslow and Dennis approach my mom.

"We know this is a difficult time, Ms. King. We want to give you the time you need, but we need to speak with you to further this investigation."

"They haven't even buried her yet, Detective," my aunt begins to argue.

"I am certainly not saying this needs to be done today. I know how delicate this situation is. I would just like to know when you think would be a good time for us to meet, Ms. King," he replies.

"Tomorrow," my mom answers.

"Carol, don't you think you should give yourself a little more time?" my aunt asks.

"No," my mom answers. "This is too important to wait on. Every day is another day that the man who did this gets to live without any consequences for his actions. I want him caught immediately. So, we'll talk tomorrow."

"Would the morning or afternoon work best for you, Ms. King?" Winslow asks, his notebook at the ready.

My mom sighs and rubs her eyes. "Afternoon, I suppose. I feel as if I could sleep for a week straight."

"You're sure tomorrow is best?" Winslow asks.

My mom pulls back her shoulders and holds her head high. "Yes, Detective. I won't lay around while that man is still out there. I want to do whatever I can."

"Okay," Winslow agrees. "We will see you tomorrow afternoon then. Around one o'clock? You have my card. Call me if you need to change it to another time or day."

My mom nods and lowers herself into my aunt's car. Winslow and Dennis wave them off then get in their car and drive off as well.

I scan around looking for Art. He's under the arch of the cemetery entrance, leaning against the wall in front of the gate. He looks like he's deep in some unpleasant thoughts but perks up when he notices me coming near.

"You're incredible, you know that?" he asks.

The compliment takes me off guard, but of course, I know what he's referring to. We are finally alone and able to discuss what I did at the funeral home. He's wasting no time.

"I don't know how I did it. I was just really angry," I say.

"Maybe strong emotions are the key," Art replies.

"I was feeling plenty of strong emotions in there," I say, pointing into the cemetery. "I wasn't able to give my mom another sign though."

"It'll take some trial and error, but I think you could do it again," he says. I can hear the confidence he has in me, and it makes me nervous. I've always been wary of praise because you can easily disappoint when someone has high opinions of you.

"What if I can't?" I ask. "What if it was just a fluke?"

He catches the apprehension in my voice and smiles. "It's still incredible that you managed it in the first place. No worries if it doesn't happen again. I'm not hoping for anything in particular. I just think it's really cool."

I relax and ask, "Well, are you going to try? If the theory is simply letting a strong emotion flood through you, both of us could keep trying."

"I thought about that, but I don't know if I could force an emotion strong enough," Art replies. "I mean, your anger came from something directly affecting you in the present. It didn't come from memories or just focusing hard enough. I suppose it could still be worth a shot though."

"How about we go to my mom's place? I think she left my room how it was before I moved out. We could practice there," I suggest.

"Fine by me," Art agrees. "Shall we walk or fly?"

"Fly? Is that what you call it? Seems more like teleportation to me," I say.

"Flying just sounds more fun," Art replies and shoots me a dorky smile.

"Well, alright, Clark Kent," I say with a chuckle. I hold my hand out to him. "Let's take flight." He chuckles too and takes my hand.

I close my eyes on his beaming smile and open them to my old bedroom. The way time seems to have stayed still here for four years floors me. I'm not sure why, since I assumed Mom had left everything as it was, but actually seeing it all just as I left it has me wanting to cry.

Well, things aren't exactly the same. I notice papier-mâché strips and slightly imperfect tiger lilies scattered around the floor. I sit down amongst them and reach for one of the flowers. My fingers pass through it. I sigh and gaze at it. The meticulously crafted petals are crumpled and creased as if attempted a few different times. Finally finished, but left out of the final bouquet because of its rumpled nature.

Still, it was made by my mother, just like all the other ones. I conjure up an image of her sitting here, surrounded by crafting material, tears falling uncontrollably and adding to the complicated nature of papier-mâché and origami. Still, she kept folding and twisting and shaping these simple pages of colored paper, so thin that her tears probably ruined several sheets. No matter how many mistakes were made though, she kept going. Her determination and stubbornness clearly trumped her grief. I saw the final bouquet. They were perfect. Yet, at this moment, that crumpled, abandoned flower a few inches away from me seems like the best of the bunch. It wears the marks of her willpower on its petals for me to see. *Look, this is how much your mother loves you. See how many times she opened me back up in order to get each fold just right so she could make you a bouquet of unflawed flowers? Every crease and crumpled edge are acts of determined love, a mother's love.*

She must have sat here for hours. Her fingers, back, legs, and butt becoming cramped, numb, or sore. All of her discomfort and inevitable frustration so that I could have a bouquet of my favorite flowers that will take a little longer to decompose than normal flowers would. So that I could have something made by her own hands to take with me.

It feels like a stone is lodged in my throat, but my eyes stay stubbornly dry. Now I'm terribly sad about what my mom is having to go through and angry that my intangible body won't let me cry for her.

I let out an exasperated huff and steel myself. I don't let myself think about it. Quickly, I snatch the flower from its place on the floor. It stays in my closed fist for a glorious ten seconds before it falls through.

"Holy shit, Hannah! This is amazing!" Art exclaims.

His outburst startles me at first, causing me to jump, but his excitement is contagious. I smile up at him.

"How did you feel before it happened this time?" he asks.

"Well, at first I was thinking of my mom sitting here making these flowers. It made me incredibly sad, made me want to cry. When I remembered I'm seemingly incapable of crying, it made me a bit angry. I didn't give myself time to overthink it. I just reached out and grabbed it," I answer with a shrug.

Art moves his shoulders in an exaggerated shrug, mocking me a little. He is still directing a massive smile my way. He laughs and shakes his head at me. "You need to give yourself some more credit, Hannah. This is so exciting!"

"It was only for like ten seconds," I point out, but I am beginning to feel a bit proud of myself under his constant praise.

"That's ten more than I could do!" Art replies.

"You haven't tried," I remind him.

He deflates with a sigh. I may have caught an eye roll too. "Alright, alright, I'll give it a try," he concedes.

He sits across from me with the flower on the floor between us. He stares at it for a while then glances up at me, doubt flooding his eyes.

"Just try not to think too much about the actual act of picking it up. Think of something that affects you strongly. Focus on the emotion then grab it quick, like a sneak attack," I say.

He nods and closes his eyes. As the moments tick by, I notice the subtle changes in his facial muscles. At first the muscles in his face are tight with concentration, but they slowly soften into something more tender.

Suddenly, his eyes shoot open, and his hand darts forward. He tries to wrap his fingers around the stem, but they pass through it effortlessly. I look up with an apologetic look on my face, but his smile is already returning.

"Oh well," he shrugs.

"Were you thinking of the kids at St. Jude's?" I ask, to which I receive a nod of approval. "Maybe you need to think of something more personal, something that affects you more directly."

A hint of a deeper pain glints in his eyes. He quickly looks away and plasters on a smile. "I think I just don't have the same touch as you do," he says, then genuinely chuckles. He looks back at me with his fake smile morphing into a real one. "Literally! Get it? I don't have the touch." Now he is giggling uncontrollably.

I can't fight the bubbles of mirth rising in my stomach as I listen to his laughter. "You're such a dork," I manage to say before I too succumb to the giggle fits.

We laugh longer than the joke merited, but it's a much-needed break from the doom and gloom feeling that has been surrounding me. Letting go of my confusion, anxieties, and sadness to laugh with someone who I know needs it as much as I do is extremely uplifting. Art may always wear happiness on his face, but this is a different level. This is a release. I see something inside of him unclench and realize I never would have truly understood the effort it has taken him to keep his cheery disposition shifted into high gear if we never had this moment.

Art takes a deep breath and releases it, humor still leaking out in fading giggles. "Feels like it's been ages since I laughed like that," he says.

"Me too, honestly," I reply. "I definitely never laughed like that with Christine and Shelley. Jules and I had our moments, but things were strained between us this past year." Some of my humor drains out of me when I say those words.

Art must have noticed because he changes the subject by asking, "And what about with Bobbi?"

A smile blooms on my face immediately. I reply, "Oh God, Bobbi and I were always laughing so hard we'd cry, clinging to each other the whole time. I couldn't tell you what any of it was about. Still, I remember how it always felt."

"Like what?" Art asks after a moment of silence.

"Like ... I was home," I reply. Suddenly, I realize ditching Bobbi was the stupidest thing I'd ever done in my life. I thought I had to abandon her in order to find where I truly belonged, but I had already found it. I was just too caught up in the things I didn't have and thought I couldn't have if I continued living the same way.

"This past year I began to wonder if I had made the wrong decision, or if maybe I just went about it all wrong," I admit. "I wanted to reach out to Bobbi, but it's like I didn't know how to anymore. Maybe that's why I started teasing her. I guess I'm no better than a little boy who bullies the girl he likes because he doesn't understand his emotions yet."

"Well, nothing you did or said to her seems to have shaken her belief that you love her. So try not to dwell on what you can't go back and erase. It'll just make you miserable," Art says.

I smile at him gratefully then sit in silence for a moment before saying, "It was interesting seeing her and Julien talking. It made me feel both happy and incredibly stupid."

"Why stupid?" Art asks.

"I hid my past from Julien because I thought he wouldn't like the person I was or the people I hung out with, but hearing them talk, it all became so obvious. I had stereotyped Julien and modeled myself into what I believed to be a match for him, then I ignored any hint he had a personality that didn't match with what I had initially assumed. I was worried that, if I believed he would accept me as I was, I would tell the truth only to be proven wrong, and he'd reject me or be angry with me. At the time, it felt like an impossible puzzle, but now, it's clearly all so ridiculous!" I exclaim.

After a beat of silence I add, "Did that make sense?"

"Yeah," Art says, breaking free from his thoughtful trance. "It's just … you keep mentioning that you changed yourself. How exactly did you do that? What did you change?"

"I partied more, acted a lot bitchier, never talked about my interest in stuff like forensic science, criminology, Stephen King, or science fiction," I answer.

"So it was subtle things," he replies. "It was more omission than a complete metamorphosis. From what your mom said about your temper tantrums, it sounds like you did have a good amount of attitude to begin with. Maybe you tuned it up—at least around the evil stepsisters—and made the choice to direct it at people more often, but we can all be assholes sometimes. Like you said, we can all revert back to our toddler days where we would lash out because we didn't understand our emotions."

"I … I guess you're right," I say. I didn't necessarily act different. I just hollowed myself out, removing Bobbi and all my interests, because I thought Julien would be into the Barbie doll type—ditzy and dependent. I felt like I made a drastic change that I couldn't come back from because I lost my identity. I emptied it all out and tried to fill myself back up just with Julien and partying with Christine and Shelley, but that was never going to be enough. I made it to where being Julien's girlfriend and Christine and Shelley's little pet was my entire personality. Being friends with Bobbi had been a major part of my life, but it wasn't the only thing in my life. I had dreams and aspirations, which Bobbie listened to and encouraged. Christine and Shelley wouldn't have understood or cared at all about any of the things I wanted, and I didn't even let Julien try because I had convinced myself that he wouldn't either.

"What's going on in that head of yours?" Art asks, breaking me out of my daze.

I open my mouth only for a sharp laugh to bubble out. I wouldn't even know where to start to try to explain everything I just realized. Instead I reply, "You just helped me realize exactly why I was feeling like an untethered astronaut drifting and spinning around in space. I've been unable to tell what's right-side-up from upside-down but suddenly it all makes sense."

"You're welcome," Art says with a pleased smile.

"Don't let it go to your head, dork," I tease.

"Didn't we just establish you are also a dork?" Art teases back.

"Doesn't make you less of one," I reply with a wink.

The corner of his mouth twitches into a smirk which he tries to hide. He points down at a black marker on the floor beside him.

"If I could pick this up, I'd throw it at you," he says. To which I simply reply by sticking my tongue out at him. His smile doesn't leave his face, and I smile brightly back at him.

12

My mom didn't sleep in. It's seven o'clock in the morning, and I hear her in the kitchen. She brews a strong pot of coffee, the aromatic bitterness nearly making my mouth water. She waits in a daze by the pot as it brews and mechanically pours herself a cup when it's finished. Then she sits at the table and drinks it slowly. Every movement is so methodical, but I can tell that her attention is not on what her hands are doing. Her eyes have a glazed, faraway look. She's moving through muscle memory.

I suddenly feel the immense weight of loneliness in these actions. She's gone through this exact same routine every morning for so long, not a single distraction to avert her attention for even a moment, that she could probably do the whole thing blindfolded and not make a single mistake. Then, after every perfect execution, she sits at the table with only empty chairs for company. How many mornings has she sat alone in this kitchen, quietly sipping her coffee, since I moved out? Four years' worth of lonely mornings spread out before me, and my heart aches sharply. I seat myself on the chair to her right and wish for her eyes to show some form of life.

I do see something shifting in her eyes once she's about halfway done with her cup. In those placid blue pools it's as if I can see a part of herself swimming towards consciousness from some deep, hidden cave she dwells in when she's alone. I also get the feeling she retreats there often these days and, if the escapes become habitual, she may lose the ability to breach the surface again. Just the thought of her always wearing this comatose expression, walking around like a zombie as her muscles jerk her around in a sad and dull performance of her day-to-day activities, makes me spiral into panic. I scan the room nervously, trying to see if there is anything I can use to send her some sort of message or to at least announce my presence.

Before I can come up with a plan my mom is up from her chair and heading down the hallway leading to the bedrooms and baths. She goes into my bedroom, and I follow.

She stands in the doorway for several moments. Her eyes scan the room, sometimes catching and holding on a certain item before drifting away again to take in the whole space. Then, she looks down at the litter of papier-mâché and used, balled up tissue paper.

"Oh, Hannah," she croaks. "Look what a mess I've left in your room."

There's a fleeting moment where her face tightens, most likely thinking about how I'm never going to be using this room again, but she shakes it off and begins picking up the mess. Using a small trashcan from beside my bed, she stuffs in all the trash and empties it into the larger can in the kitchen. Then she drags in the vacuum cleaner and powers it up.

She's beginning her second pass around the room with the vacuum when my aunt shows up in the doorway looking frazzled and concerned. She calls my mom's name until she shuts the vacuum off and looks at her.

"Sweetheart, what are you doing?" my aunt asks. She speaks in her soft mom voice, the voice used when you don't want your child to think you're angry with them but you think they need to stop whatever it is they are doing.

My mom looks quizzically at the vacuum and around the room, then back at my aunt. "I left a mess," she answers.

"It's seven-thirty in the morning," my aunt replies.

"Oh, right," my mom says, moving closer to full consciousness. "I'm sorry I woke you."

"Carol," my aunt tuts and hurries in to wrap her arms around my mom. She sits on my bed, guiding my mom to do the same. "I don't care about that. I just think you should be resting. Are you okay?"

My mom grips my aunt's hand like it's a life raft and says, "Yes, I am. As okay as I can be at least. I promise."

"Okay, I really think you should get more rest before those detectives come by later," my aunt says.

"I made coffee already," my mom replies with a small, apologetic smile. "I won't be able to fall back asleep."

My aunt sighs and strokes my mom's hair. "Make enough for two?" she asks.

"Sorry, I'm used to making just enough for one. I can make another pot for you," my mom answers, already getting to her feet.

My aunt hops up and darts out the room first, calling back to my mom, "Don't even think about it. I can do it myself."

A faint smile flickers across my mom's face but fades quickly. She takes a final look around the room before letting out a shaky sigh and following my aunt back to the kitchen.

My mom takes her abandoned cup to the sink and reaches for the soap and sponge which my aunt snatches from her.

"Leave it in the sink," my aunt instructs. "I'll wash everything after I'm finished with my cup."

"What do you expect me to do then?" my mom huffs and tosses her hands up.

My aunt points at the table and says, "Sit and talk with me. Is that an acceptable use of your time?"

"Of course, it is," my mom says. She softens, allowing herself to relax, and sinks into one of the chairs.

"Good," my aunt says, settling into the chair next to my mom with a fresh cup of coffee in hand. "I was beginning to think you were starting to wish I was back in Colorado."

"Not at all," my mom replies emphatically, reaching out and grasping my aunt's hand. "I'm so glad you're here, Claire."

"I'm right where I want to be," Aunt Claire replies. She squeezes my mom's hand and smiles warmly at her.

They talk for a time about Aunt Claire's kids and her husband. From there, they move on to her job and how my mom's bakery has been doing. Then they get into plans for the day. While Aunt Claire is cooking eggs, my mom is asking about lunch.

"What do you think you'll want?" she asks my aunt. "Come up with something so I can write up a grocery list."

My aunt turns to her with a mischievous smile and says, "Let's just be bad and get Checkers. It's been ages since I had a burger from there."

My mom chuckles and replies, "They always were your favorite. You used to badger mom for Checkers at least once a week."

"And I'll badger you if I have to," my aunt says, and I know she's not joking.

"We can get burgers," my mom says, giving in. She has an amused look on her face, and her eyes are gleaming with humor instead of glazed over.

My worry from earlier is dissipating. I'm extremely grateful for my aunt and her ability to draw my mom out from those depths. A bit of the panic comes back when I think of how my aunt will need to leave in two more days, but I try not to dwell on it. Right now, I just want to enjoy and appreciate the fact that my mom is smiling again.

"Yay!" my aunt exclaims and does a little victory dance as she walks to my mom's side with two plates of eggs. "Get up! Since we're going to be bad later, we may as well start now. We'll go eat on the couch and watch something ridiculous, like Pawn Stars or Steampunk'd, until those detectives come by. No arguing!"

"Fine," my mom sighs and rolls her eyes. "You better not get egg all over my couch though."

They settle on Steampunk'd, agreeing it seems like the more ridiculous of the two programs my aunt mentioned. As entertaining as their commentary on the show is, I decide I'd rather have a walk around the town with Art. With my mom joking and laughing with her sister, I feel okay about leaving for a while. I tell him to follow me and head out of the house.

Walking down the street together, Art says, "Your mom and your aunt seem like really fun people to be around. You must have laughed nonstop around them."

"My aunt has always been the crazier of the two, just the nature of older sisters versus younger sisters I suppose, but my mom absolutely was always a blast to be around. My aunt moved to Colorado before I was born, so I didn't get to see her a whole lot, but she invited us all the time. She has a lakeside house with a speedboat and waterboards. I was always super excited to go for a visit. How many times a year we went depended on finances and how long my mom was willing to be away from the bakery. Bobbi and her mom came with us a few times. I remember a time when we were younger, Bobbi and I got on our moms' shoulders to play chicken in the lake. My aunt came up between us and shoved both of us off our perches, then we started an epic splash fight. She was merciless. My mom and Ms. Jean had to gang up on her. Once all four of us were pummeling her with splash after splash, she finally accepted defeat."

Art is smiling distantly as I recall the memory. I know he's listening, but I can also tell he's in the midst of something a lot farther away from me and this conversation, something years in the past that is calling his name. It seems like a happy memory since the smile on his face is soft and genuine, but there is a sadness dulling his eyes. I stay silent for a while, letting him relive whatever moment from his past came forward from the fog of repression.

"We had a lake house in Oregon we used for vacations," Art begins. "My dad always cooked breakfast when we stayed at the lake. My mom was a full-time parent, so she was the one to get up early and cook breakfast for my dad before he went off to work and for us before school. When we were away, my dad wanted her to relax. He did everything for her, all the cooking, all the cleaning, and especially all the looking after us. She never slept in though or kept inside for some peace and quiet when we went out to the lake. She was always right there by my dad's side. The mornings were my favorite because my dad would sing to her as he cooked, Italian love songs, and they would dance."

He breaks from his narrative and begins to sing.

Che cosa c'è?

C'è che mi sono innamorato di te.

C'è che ti voglio tanto bene.

E il mondo mi appartiene.

Il mondo mio che è fatto solo di te.

I don't know what the words mean, but his voice is like the rise and fall of waves in the ocean. The flow of emotion rocks me gently like a baby in a cradle, lulling me to a state of complete peace and safety. Even if he hadn't specified Italian love songs, I would have known it was one. Listening to him, I feel as if I'm being embraced and caressed. I swear I feel a small blossoming of warmth try to unfurl in my chest, but the verse ends and the sensation follows suit, leaving me wondering if it was even there to begin with.

I take a deep breath, only now realizing I had been holding it in. I do my best to control my voice, hoping it doesn't come out squeaky or shaky. I tell him, "Wow, that was beautiful. You didn't mention you had such a talent for singing, and in Italian! Are you fluent?"

"No," Art chuckles. "I just memorized certain songs my dad would sing often, and I liked listening to some on my own time. It is a beautiful language so the music always soothed me. I can loosely translate most Italian I hear, but I don't think I'd be completely reliable if you dropped us anywhere in Italy."

"Well, what's the loose translation of the one you just sang?" I ask.

"Something like 'What's the matter? It's that I'm so in love with you. You are my world,'" he answers.

I smile. "That's really sweet. Was that his go-to serenade?"

He looks at me with a wistful smile softening his eyes and nods. "Mom loved it. She was like butter in his arms. He'd hold her, dancing in slow circles in front of the stove, and she'd look into his eyes the whole time. The look on both of their faces was ... well, it's what I think of when I hear 'pure love.' We did what kids do when faced with the evidence of how much their parents love each other, gagging noises and begging for them not to act like that while we eat, but I always thought it was really sweet. I dreamed of being that type of husband, feeling that kind of love."

I wonder if it's the unfairness of the situation, that his life was cut short before he could have that experience, or if it's the recollection of his mother, his father, or even both of them that makes the memories of those mornings so heavy with melancholy.

My legs have been on autopilot since my brain has been occupied with sharing lake house memories. I glance around to get my bearings and see the park across the street. I point it out to Art, and we both check the street for passing cars before remembering they would just drive right through us, which we joke about as we head toward the park.

"What if it flattened us like in a cartoon?" I ask.

"Then we drift upwards with the wind and pop back into our regular shape," Art adds, and we both laugh.

"Road Runner rules, huh? Guess we should watch for falling anvils instead of cars," I say.

"I hated that cartoon so much," Art replies.

"He is a very annoying bird so that's understandable," I say.

"I was more into Scooby-Doo," he says.

"Oh my God, me too!" I exclaim. "Man, it's been so long since I've even thought of that one. It was definitely my comfort show when I was younger though."

Sitting at a picnic table in the park, Art and I talk about every show from our childhood we can remember and some more recent ones that really hooked us. He binge-watched shows old and new when he was in the hospital, so he has a lot more in his memory bank than I do, but he reminds me of several I hadn't thought of in years. It's almost therapeutic to sit in the park and have a pointless conversation, to focus on the simple topic of our favorite forms of entertainment. We continue to do so, moving from shows to movies to music, until kids with their moms in tow start to stream into the park.

Our conversation tapers off as we watch the kids run, climb, and tumble around the playground, occasionally running to their mothers for sips from a juice box or to ask them "Are you watching? Did you see what I did?" to which they reply with an enthusiastic nod and rain praises down on their child.

"Simpler times, eh?" Art says.

"Yeah, no kidding," I agree as we watch a kid attempt a cartwheel that looks more like a sideways crab walk. The kid's mom still claps proudly.

"That's the mark of a good mother, wouldn't you say?" Art asks. He turns to me with a good-humored, lopsided grin on his face which draws out my own smile.

"Was your mom like that?" I ask.

His demeanor immediately changes. The grin dips down then tries to right itself, but it's like the corners of his mouth have grown heavy. Every muscle in his body tightens as if clenching around a hidden item not yet ready to be revealed. His energy dims, drawing back into his body to hide from a potential threat to its vitality. I feel the withdrawal in my own body too.

When Art feels safe and comfortable, his energy is a revitalizing source that flows out from him, wraps around you, and whispers that everything will be okay. His presence is like a weighted blanket that smothers all anxiety. So, when he draws into himself as he is doing now, it's like something as vital as oxygen has been sucked out of the air, leaving a vacuum in its place that is hungry for energy, but no one else has enough liveliness to possibly fill that void.

I grasp for anything to say that could reverse what I did, something that might draw him back into the easy rapport we just had.

Before I can come up with anything, he says with some hesitation, "Yeah, she was. Mostly, she was."

I can't get a read on what the core issue is when it comes to his mother. He didn't seem wound up like this when he mentioned her in connection to his dad. When he spoke of the two of them, it was more nostalgic and melancholy. Speaking of her in isolation though, it's like he's walking around in a field with thousands of hidden land mines lying in wait.

I feel like backpedaling wouldn't be very effective in this situation, so I shift the conversation at least slightly away from his mother by asking, "And what about your dad?"

He loosens up a bit as he answers, "Dad was definitely like that. He was incredibly even-tempered. Hardly anything could shake that man. Even when me and my brothers would get too rough with each other, I don't remember him ever raising his voice at us. He had a way of dispelling tension so smoothly. It was just impossible to keep your anger intact when faced with his unshakeable calm, and his capacity for empathy was inspiring."

"He sounds like the perfect dad," I say, and I genuinely mean it. I wouldn't say my dad was the worst dad anyone could have, but I think it's fair to say anyone could see that he would never win Dad of the Year. The person Art described sounds like an angel. Honestly, it seems like his dad had the same energy that I feel in Art. Clearly, his dad was the biggest influence to who he has become. For that, I feel indebted to him because I have no idea what I'd be doing right now if it wasn't for Art.

"I think his personality rubbed off on you quite a bit," I tell him. "Sounds to me like you're describing yourself."

He scoffs but in an amused, sort of incredulous, way. "I'm nowhere near as uplifting as my dad was. He was on a whole other level."

"You must miss him a lot," I say. It feels like a stupid response because it's obvious that he does. The man was his idol. Who wouldn't miss the person who shaped them? I just couldn't think of anything else to say.

"When I first realized I was stuck in some sort of limbo, I called out to him constantly, wondering if there was perhaps some sort of spiritual connection that could be made, so he could find me and take me with him," Art says and takes a deep, steading breath before continuing. "Except, he moved on years ago. He died when I was eighteen. It was a stroke followed by a fatal heart attack, all very sudden. Then, two years later, we found out about my brain cancer. I was in and out of the hospital for two years. I spent the last five months of my life almost completely in a hospital bed, and I was torn between wishing he could be there to comfort me versus feeling like I shouldn't wish him the pain of watching his youngest son die. Either way, no matter how desperate I was for him to be there, nothing could change the fact that he wasn't and couldn't magically return just for me."

There was a lot of pain attached to the last bit of his speech, but it's clear to me he doesn't assign any guilt to his father for not being there at the end. There was an intense feeling of loneliness to his words however that leaves me wondering, who *was* there for him?

"So, you were twenty when you were diagnosed and still got to do your treatments at St. Jude's? I thought they were a children's hospital," I ask in an attempt to begin pulling away from the more personal, emotionally painful parts of his illness. I can sense dark clouds heavy with electricity forming in his mind. I have to at least attempt to draw him away from the possible storm, and the only way I can think to do so is with distraction.

"Yeah, I think the age limits differ with each diagnosis. Like, with certain brain tumors and cancers they accept patients as old as twenty-five," he answers.

"Did you have any smoking hot nurses?" I ask in an attempt to catch him off-guard and knock those dark thoughts from his mind.

I think it may have worked because he looks at me with his lips slightly apart, then the corners of his mouth lift slowly into an amused smile. He shakes his head and says, "You are so ridiculous."

I decide to stick with it and continue, "I think it's a valid question to ask. Come on, you had to have a crush on one of them. Aren't nurses every guy's wet dream?"

"You're stereotyping," Art chides. I can hear the steady undercurrent of humor beginning to flow again in his voice and feel a sense of accomplishment.

"Are you telling me that I'm wrong? Or did you just not have a hot nurse?" I keep going.

I see a faint blush rise to his cheeks and demand to know who she was.

"Her name was Jessica," he gives in. "She had a very sunshiny personality. It was nearly impossible for me to keep brooding when she was around."

I flash him my smuggest smile and say, "I knew it. You can't hide things from me, Art. I'm like a prophet. I'll look into your soul."

He rolls his eyes then bows dramatically, even going down on one knee. "Whatever you say, your holiness."

"That would be considered overacting. I don't necessarily appreciate it, but I will accept it. You may stand," I say, trying to sound reproachful but barely able to contain my laughter.

"Well, overall, I'd say this was a nice outing," Art says as he stands. "Think we should go back? I'd say it's getting close to one o'clock."

"I think that's a good idea," I say and take the hand he extends to me.

"Shall we fly?" he asks.

"We shall," I answer and close my eyes.

Back at my mom's, Bobbi and Ms. Jean must have joined my mom and aunt for lunch. They sit in the living room. My mom and aunt on the couch, Bobbi and her mom on the flanking chairs. I notice my mom's burger lay abandoned on the table in the kitchen with only two bites taken out of it. She holds a small carton of fries in her hands on the couch, no doubt at the urging of my aunt, taking tiny nibbles when she notices her sister glancing at her.

She seems to be having trouble staying present, fighting that urge to retreat into herself to hide from her new reality. Her eyes are getting that glazed over look that had me in such a panic this morning, and I'm sure it has to do with the fact the conversation is about me. Not about what happened to me or who could have done it, just favorite memories and funny stories, but it's still a reminder that I'm no longer there and never will be again.

There is a short pause after Ms. Jean finishes a story, then my aunt says with a sigh, "God, I'm going to miss that girl."

A quiet moment of agreement passes before Ms. Jean says, "But she will always be with us. She has a place in all of our hearts."

"She's still here," my mom says, causing Ms. Jean and my aunt stiffen.

"Carolyn," Aunt Claire says softly and places a hand on my mom's arm. "Let's not do this again, sweetheart."

My mom glares at her and replies, "How can you deny it after what we all saw at the funeral home?"

"It just fell or somebody bumped into it," my aunt answers, but she sounds unconvinced by her own explanation.

"It wasn't near enough to the wall to just fall and smash against it. That vase was thrown, and you all know it. You just won't admit it," my mom argues.

"I believe you," Bobbi says.

"Bobbi!" Ms. Jean snaps.

"What?" she snaps back. "I've said this countless times, Mom. Just because you don't understand something doesn't mean it's automatically wrong. Why not let us believe? There's no harm in it."

"Yes, there is!" Ms. Jean says. "There is a process with grief. If you let yourself get stuck in one stage, especially the denial stage, it's incredibly difficult to find your way out."

My mom's face softens as she looks at Ms. Jean.

Bobbi's dad was killed in a car accident when she was about four years old. Ms. Jean had a really bad year after his passing. Very often Bobbi had to stay with relatives or with us because her mom was drunk or simply too torn apart from grief to keep an eye on her daughter. It took a wide support system and Alcoholics Anonymous to bring her back.

Bobbi and I don't remember those times since we were very young, but my mom told me about it. So, I know my mom understands where Ms. Jean is coming from, sympathizes with her, and appreciates her concern, but I can also sense that she knows this situation is different from what Ms. Jean went through. She decides not to press the issue any further and lets the room fall silent.

Her thoughts though ... her thoughts are loud, and I can suddenly hear them more clearly than I can hear the tentative beginnings of a more mundane conversation being struck up between Ms. Jean and my aunt about her family. She asks my mom if perhaps going spend some time at my aunt's or even just taking a little vacation by herself might be a good idea, and my mom smiles, nods, and says maybe, but what's really on her mind fills my ears and my heart.

Stay present. Don't let them see the cracks. Don't disappear. Focus. Keep looking at them. Keep listening to them. Don't dissociate. You need to be present. The detectives will be coming soon. The detectives, asking about Hannah, asking about Dale. Because Dale killed my baby, and I need to tell them. Killed my baby. Oh God. Hannah.

Hannah. Hannah. Hannah.

The panic grows heavy in my chest, smothering me. I pace around the room nervously, vaguely hearing Art ask me what's wrong. I wave him away and keep thinking. I stop behind the couch and consider the lamp on the end table. Trying to send her a message through lights could be explained away too easily. I don't need everyone else to see the message either. It should be something only she would see and understand that it's me.

I stare at the back of her head as I'm still standing behind her, and it hits me. Something personal and obvious that it's me. Not something she can see, but something she can feel.

When I was still living with her, if I came down the hall and saw she was sitting on the couch, I'd try to come up behind her as quietly as I could and blow on her neck to scare her. She would make this surprised squeak and swat at her neck before turning around to see me standing behind her, giggling up a storm. She'd swat at me then and tell me to stop being such a little gremlin, but she'd have a smile on her face.

Those memories mix with my mom's agonized, heartbroken internal monologue as I position myself so my face is inches from her neck. Her thoughts are tearing my heart to shreds, but I continue to listen. They make me want to scream in pain with her—for her. Instead, I purse my lips and blow air softly through them.

That same noise from my memories escapes her mouth, and her hand goes to her neck. Everyone looks to her with concern etched on their faces.

"Mosquito," she says and waves away their worry.

She keeps still, hand cradling her neck, for a couple moments longer before taking a quick peek behind her. Seeing nothing, she moves to face forward again. As she does, she catches Bobbi's eyes. They stare at each other, an understanding passing between them.

Although I'm sure Bobbi has seen me do this prank before, I don't know whether she completely understands what my mom felt. However, I can tell that she knows my mom sensed my presence, and she believes the truth of it just as much as my mom does without needing proof.

I go over to Art, who is again staring at me in pure wonder. This level of admiration makes me uncomfortable. It's starting to make me feel like I've stumbled across something I wasn't meant to. I have no clue how I'm able to do these things when he can't. It seems like there's a connection to my emotions, but I can't tell if it's because I can control and harness them or because they are completely out of control and I'm just along for the ride.

"She actually felt you! Hannah, that's beyond impressive," Art says.

"She was slipping away, starting to dissociate. I could hear her thoughts, Art. They were heartbreaking. I had to do something," I reply.

"I've actually experienced that before," Art says, and I feel a bit less like an anomaly.

"You've heard someone's thoughts?" I ask.

"Yeah, a mother's thoughts as she sat next to her sleeping kid after he went through a radiation treatment," Art answers.

"That must have been hard to hear," I say and place a hand on his forearm.

Before my hand can fall back to my side, Art catches it in his and gives it a squeeze.

"We've really been through some shit, haven't we?" Art asks.

The laughter escapes my throat before I can even think to swallow it down. Through it, I reply, "Yeah, I think that's a fair statement to make."

Art laughs along with me and says, "Understatement of the year."

"Of the century," I correct him.

I notice my hand is still enveloped in his. Just as I realize that I don't want him to let go, he does. It feels heavier somehow, so I let it drop to my side and dangle there uselessly.

When I look up at Art, he's looking at the door. I also notice Bobbi and her mother quickly gathering their things and saying hasty goodbyes. Then I hear the doorbell chime and my mom hurries to the door. I guess I missed the initial ring or knocks that grabbed Art's attention and got Bobbi and Ms. Jean on their feet.

My mom opens the door and greets Detective Winslow and Dennis.

"Sorry for the delay," she says. "We had lunch together and got to talking. Lost track of time. Come on in."

As soon as the detectives are in, Bobbi and Ms. Jean bustle out, their apologies trailing behind them. Winslow graciously assures them it was no trouble.

"Should I stay or go to my room?" Aunt Claire asks from her spot on the couch.

"We'd love for you to join us, ma'am," Detective Winslow replies.

The detectives occupy the recently vacated chairs, and my mom sits back down next to my aunt on the couch. Silence hangs in the air as Detective Winslow gets his trusty tape recorder into position and flips through his notebook to a blank page. He hits record and hurries through the introduction, marking the date and time, stating his and Dennis's names, and getting my mom and aunt to do the same.

"Ms. King, I'd like to start by asking you if Hannah seemed on edge or different in any way in the last few months perhaps?" Winslow begins.

"She didn't seem paranoid or scared, but she did seem more distant," my mom answers.

"Could you try to explain to us how that presented itself?" Winslow asks.

"Well, we were very close, Hannah and me. We talked about everything with each other. She knew nothing was completely off the table with me. All her life, she felt comfortable confiding in me about all sorts of things, but in the past few months, I felt like she was holding something back. There was definitely something on her mind that she wasn't telling me about," she explains.

"But not something she felt overly threatened by?" Dennis asks.

"I don't believe so. It was more like she was always lost in her own thoughts, not fretting but brooding maybe," she says.

"Did you ever ask her directly if something was bothering her?" Winslow asks.

"Of course," my mom answers. "Several times in fact. She would just try to pass it off as general boredom. 'Work is boring, school is boring.' That's all she'd say."

"Perhaps she was just discontent? Restless?" Winslow asks.

"I think it was a little more than that. She seemed ... lost," my mom replies.

Winslow nods, jots down a quick note, then says, "Ms. King, Bobbi Willow mentioned a man by the name of Dale. She claims to have seen this man at the bar where Hannah works the night of the crime. She told us about the incident at the barbeque. Would you be able to tell us yourself so we can corroborate her story?"

At the sound of his name, my mom goes rigid. Her face creases with the intensity of her scowl, but she manages to tell the whole story without a tremor in her voice. By the end, Dennis is also scowling and sitting stiffly in his chair. His jaw clenching and unclenching rhythmically.

"You said Bobbi saw him at the bar. What about Julien? Did he say anything that may implicate Dale?" my mom asks.

"Mr. Stoll mentioned that he *thinks* the man knew Hannah personally, but I don't think it's wise of you to put all your eggs in one basket just yet, ma'am. We'd also advise you not to mention your suspicions to anyone, and we asked the same from Ms. Willow. If he is guilty, we don't want him catching on that we're on his scent. If he isn't guilty, we don't want to make him a pariah. Okay?" Winslow asks.

The conviction is still prevalent in my mom's eyes, but she nods her agreement to his terms.

"Now, tell me a bit about Dale. Whatever you know. Last name, where he lives, what he does, stuff like that," Winslow says.

"It's Dale Evans. I believe it was about eight years ago he moved out to the edge of town. He has a sort of ranch out there. It's small, or at least I think it is. I think he only keeps a few chickens, a horse, a cow, maybe a goat or two. He quit working after his parents passed away. They left him a fair amount of money. That's about all I know. We didn't really keep in touch. Only reason I've kept up with him that much is from the grapevine, you know. People around here like talking about what everyone else is doing," my mom says.

"Yes, I suppose I've noticed that," Winslow agrees. "We really appreciate you taking the time to answer our questions." Then, he turns to my aunt and asks, "Do you have anything you'd like to add, ma'am?"

My aunt, who was mainly emotional support until this moment, is a bit surprised to be addressed but replies, "No sir, I didn't really see Hannah all that often. I live in Colorado. It's been a while since she came with Carol to visit."

"That's alright," Winslow says and plucks a business card from his briefcase which he extends out to my aunt. "I'll give you my card anyway, just in case. You never know what might be helpful. Call if you think of anything, anytime."

My aunt takes the card and nods. She gives my mom's hand a final squeeze then heads to the kitchen.

As Winslow packs his things back into his briefcase, my mom asks, "What's next, Detective?"

"We have people currently working on getting DNA samples from every male that was at all close to Hannah. That means neighbors, coworkers, classmates. The DNA findings came back to us today, no matches in our system, so we need to cross-reference as many people as we can. Dennis and I plan to personally visit Dale and attempt to obtain a DNA sample. If he refuses, we'll need more evidence than we have to legally force him into providing a sample," Winslow explains.

"If he refuses, wouldn't that be a clear sign of guilt?" my mom asks.

"It would be another reason for suspicion, but it wouldn't be conclusive. Nothing we have on him as of yet is conclusive," Winslow answers. In response to my mom's huff of annoyance, he continues, "Please be patient with us Ms. King. I know it's hard. I know you want justice for your girl, but try to remember that we want the same thing. We will find the man who did this, and we will put him behind bars. That is a promise."

"A conclusive promise?" my mom asks.

Winslow smiles and says, "A hundred percent conclusive."

She accompanies the detectives to the door, thanks them, and asks them to do better than their best for her baby. They tell her they will, then the door shuts. Mom turns around to see Aunt Claire walking up to her with a glass of water and a pill on her outstretched hand.

She stares at the painkiller for a moment before looking back at my aunt and asking, "How did you know I was starting to get a headache?"

"Uh, how do you think I know?" my aunt asks as if the answer is so simple a raccoon would be able to guess it. "You're my sister, Carol. I know you better than I know myself. Take it."

My mom smiles and does what she's told. After a few gulps, she places the cup on the end table and sinks into my aunt's embrace.

"I love you, Claire," my mom says through shaky breaths.

"I love you too, sweetheart," Aunt Claire replies and strokes my mom's hair as the tears begin to fall.

I leave them in each other's arms, and Art follows me outside.

"What now?" he asks.

I'm about to tell him that I think we should follow the detectives when the sky begins to change rapidly from bright daylight to the softening light of evening to the dark of night and back again, over and over. I look to him in confusion, meaning to ask him if he knows what's going on, but I'm distracted by the way the shadows play across his face. How they, at times, accentuate certain features—his nose, his cheekbones, his deep-set eyes, his lips.

"Don't worry, I've seen this before. Time works funny here sometimes, speeds up like this. It's a long one this time," Art explains without me asking anything.

The cycle abruptly ends during an evening phase, and there is now a thin layer of snow settled on the ground. The light is fading, leaving everything looking soft around the edges. Usually, this time of day always made me feel peaceful. In this moment, however, I only feel apprehensive.

"I wasn't counting. How many was that? It seemed like a lot," I say with a considerable amount of concern thickening my voice.

"I think it was about twenty-eight," Art answers.

"Jesus, nearly a whole month just went by?" I ask.

"Maybe they got him already?" Art suggests, but the way his voice pitched up slightly on the last word, like it was a question, shows he doubts it as much as I do.

"Shit," I mutter. What am I meant to do now? How do I catch up on what's been going on with the investigation? If there even is anything to catch up on ... but I can't start thinking like that. I just need to go to the command center. If I find Winslow and Dennis, I'm sure some events from the last month will be mentioned. Even if they aren't, I can at least find out what's being done right now.

"Let's go find the two bloodhounds," I say to Art, holding my hand out towards him.

He looks at me quizzically for a moment before he gets my meaning. A smile lifts up his face, and he chuckles as he takes my hand.

I close my eyes and bring the sleuthing duo to mind. I picture them both as I nearly always see them—Dennis pacing around in a circle like a caged wildcat and Winslow with his tape recorder and notepad.

I take a peek and see we are now in a decently-sized office, one wall covered by filing cabinets. A desk at the other end of the room faces the cabinets. Winslow sits behind it, and Dennis is slouched in a chair in front of it. His head is hung so low his chin is nearly touching his chest.

"We've stagnated. We've got nothing, not even a tiny shred of DNA from him that we can cross-reference. Only other people who refused to give us DNA were some boys from the college whose Mommies told them they didn't have to, or who just wanted to give us a headache, and an elderly neighbor we know damn well couldn't have been our guy anyway. We know it was Dale, but that bastard gets to stay out there, free as a bird, because we've stagnated," Dennis says.

Winslow slams a hand against his desk, causing me, Art, and Dennis to jump. Then he puts on his Superior Officer voice and berates Dennis.

"You think I'm not aware of the situation? You don't think I'm upset about it, pissed even? Of course I am, but wagging my tongue about it or sulking over it won't do a damn thing to change it! If we really want to get him, we've got to do it right, son! Don't you dare go getting your hopes down and let it affect your work. We need to stay sharp and stay on this guy's ass. Everything shows this was not particularly a planned kill. Planned abduction and sexual assault certainly, but not the killing. Which means he'll make a mistake. Guys like him always do. Toxicology reports are still coming in since I told them to check for numerous forms of tranquilizers and anything else they could think of that may be relevant. Something will hit, Dennis. We've just got to stay patient. Understand me?"

Dennis finally lifts his head and meets Winslow's eyes. He searches them for something, or perhaps tries to absorb some of the strength he sees in that gaze. Solemnly, he nods in agreement.

"Sorry," he sighs and rubs his hands down his face. "It won't happen again."

"Look, son, I'm sorry I snapped," Winslow says genuinely, not just trying to smooth things over. "You can talk to me about your frustrations. I feel them too. I just don't want to see you bloodied and bruised by them. You get me?"

"Yeah, I get you," Dennis says. He's sitting up straight now, morphing back into his stoic persona.

"Emotions and tensions are running high. I apologize. No hard feelings?" Winslow asks and extends his arm out toward Dennis.

A small grin tugs at Dennis's mouth, and he grasps Winslow's hand. He gives it a firm shake and says, "No hard feelings, partner."

Dennis leaves after that, so I assume my case is on pause at the moment with nothing much to report from the past month. It's what I expected, but I had allowed myself to hope for at least a little something more than nothing, so I am still a bit disappointed.

I sulk over to the window and see a small but pretty courtyard below. Art and I go down and sit at a round, cement table next to a fountain and a very dead rose bush covered in frost. The fountain gurgles softly, soothing my nerves. I sit for several moments with my eyes closed and listen.

I imagine myself as a pixie, too small for the human eye to register. I take to the sky and ride the wind currents to my favorite little brook which babbles a welcome to me as I approach. I dive into waters that look as vast as one of the Great Lakes to my small eyes, and when I fly back into the air, I flutter my wings so fast every drop of moisture clinging to them rains down on whatever is below me. I shower tiny frogs and growing flowers as I laugh from pure happiness from up above.

When I was younger, I used to imagine myself as all sorts of creatures—fairies, mermaids, unicorns, dragons, vampires, you name it. I haven't gone deep into a fantasy like this in quite a while, so the daydream surprises me a bit. I'm grateful for my intact imagination though because it actually helps my mood immensely.

I let it fade and turn my attention to Art, who is looking at me patiently and with a softness in his eyes that makes me feel like my stomach is made of Jell-O.

"Where were you?" he asks.

"In a silly fantasy," I answer with a smile on my face and in my voice. "Now, I think I'm ready to come up with my next move."

"What're you thinking?"

"I should check on Jules. I probably should have wanted to long before now, but that house. I don't know if I can go back yet."

"That's completely understandable. I know you love him ..." Did I hear a note of disappointment in his voice? I try to detect another subtle flex in his cadence as he continues, "But some things take time. If you're ready, that's great. If not, don't beat yourself up about it."

"Do I love him?" I ask myself aloud. "Have I ever? I wonder ..." Art waits patiently for me to continue. "For several months, maybe even the whole year, I found myself questioning everything. I cared about Jules, still do, but I wasn't sure that I could really say I was in love with him. Being with him was more like a goal or a way to reach my other goals."

"Which were?" Art urges me on.

I laugh from the irony of it. "To see the world and feel all the excitement it had to give, and Jules' life seemed so full of excitement. He raced motorcycles, and we took our trips on his. He drove the winding roads along the mountains like a pro. Watching the world whiz by, it was breathtaking. Except, I started to think that I was getting love and excitement mixed up. I started to wonder if I was with him only so that I could hold on to that feeling of heart-thumping exhilaration, and I knew that wouldn't be fair for him if I was."

"I'm assuming you never came to a solid conclusion?" Art asks.

"I didn't then, but I think I have since," I answer.

"So, what would you say now?" Art asks, and I again wonder if I'm hearing something in his voice that may not be there at all. I think I detect a bit of hope hiding in that question.

"I would say he's a really, really great guy, and I care about him a lot, but I'm not in love with him. I do think I was at the beginning, but it faded into something that no longer filled my heart quite as much."

"And that's okay, Hannah. That's life," Art says.

I smile at him and reply, "I would still like to check on him."

Art nods and asks, "Shall we go now?"

He extends his arms across the table, palms up and fingers wiggling. I lay my arms with palms facing down over his, grasping him just below the elbow. His hands gently wrap around my arms the same way from underneath, and butterflies begin to flutter around in my stomach. I try not to think about what that means as I close my eyes and bring Jules into my mind.

Just as I set our destination in my mind's eye, I feel buds of heat flicker into existence where the tips of Art's fingers touch my skin. The sensation is gone in the next instant when I open my eyes to the kitchen of the house that I lived in with Jules for two years.

Art's hands fall away from me, and he takes a look around the room. I keep looking at him, but I can't determine if he felt those little pricks of warmth as well.

"Your friend is here too," he says, and I put my wonderings to the side for now.

The layout of this half of the house is very open. The kitchen and the living room are separated only by a long counter and a couple feet of space empty of any furnishings other than two potted plants at either end of the room which look in dire need of water.

We can see and hear Julien and Bobbi from where they sit on the couch in the living room from our spot in the kitchen, but we both move closer anyway. I see Julien is in quite an anxious but also angry state. He's fidgeting with the three rings that were almost always on his fingers, and his legs are bouncing jerkily, both indications that he's anxious. He's also huffing a lot as he talks, running his hands roughly through his hair, and rolling his shoulders erratically—signs he's angry.

"I can't believe they still haven't got this son of a bitch," he rants. "It's so damn hard to go about my life day after day like it never happened, like it doesn't matter that this guy hasn't been caught. It felt so wrong to find a new job and go back to a normal working schedule. Then, I come home to an empty bed in an empty house and feel everything from the day just drain out of me. It makes me feel so hollow and like everything I do during the day is pointless."

Bobbi puts her hand over his, calming his unconscious tic of violently digging at his cuticles. She replies, "It's good that you got a new job and get out of the house. First of all, you need the job to keep the house. Second, Hannah wouldn't want any of us to hole ourselves away to mope or gnash our teeth."

"I'm not renewing the lease," Julien says. "I don't think I'll be able to make all the bills with one meager paycheck. I can't get two jobs because I'm supposed to start night classes in the spring."

"Julien, that's great," Bobbi says. "When did you decide on that?"

"I found out I was accepted the day it happened. I was going to tell her when she got home, but we fought instead. Now, it doesn't feel right anymore to go through with it," he says.

Bobbi and I say at the same time, "Do it!"

I smile at the emergence of our mind-reading-like connection. Bobbi and I were always so in sync with each other. We had countless instances where we'd finish each other's sentences or say the same thing at the same time. This was a small one and could easily be dismissed as coincidence, but it still brought awareness to one last strong thread of our connection which I cling to greedily.

Bobbi continues, "She'd want us to live our lives. She had so much she wanted to see and do. We should remember and honor her by going out and doing the things we want as soon as we can, since tomorrow is never truly promised. I think she would tell us that our time is too precious to be spent dwelling on horrible events from the past. It'll take us a lot of time to heal, but that's what she wants for us, to heal and continue on."

An agonized look passes over Julien's face, and he admits in a voice heavy with pain and guilt, "Bobbi, sometimes I go the whole day without thinking of her. How fucking horrible is that? Then, it all comes rushing back the second I walk in that door. And I hate the guy who took her, but I think I hate myself more."

Bobbi is shaking her head and grabs his chin to make him look at her. She looks into his eyes with sympathy but also a fierceness that always flames up inside her when someone she cares for is in trouble.

"Don't you dare say that," Bobbi says. "You are a good man, Julien. You were good to her, and you did all you could for her when she needed you. You were there for her, and you tried with everything you had in you to help her. I know it's a shitty fucking situation, I struggle with it too, but it is in no way shape or form your fault, Julien. Please, don't keep torturing yourself with those thoughts."

Bobbi starts to cry halfway through her speech. A steady stream leaks from her eyes, blazing a path down each cheek. Julien looks on with glassy eyes.

The room falls silent as they stare at each other, each reflecting concern for the other in their eyes and body language. Julien wipes at one of the rivers of tears on Bobbi's cheek before suddenly pulling her in and kissing her gently.

For a moment, Bobbi melts into his embrace. She kisses him back with a quiet passion that could easily build into a scorching blaze. She must have felt that heat rising, because she hurriedly pushes away from him and gets to her feet. She touches a shaky hand to her lips and stares at him.

Jules breathes heavily. He rubs his hands down his face and says, "Fuck, I'm so sorry. What the fuck was I thinking? Bobbi, I'm really sorry."

Bobbi has her breath and her wits back. She immediately goes back to his side and puts her hands over his.

"It's okay, Julien. I wanted it too. I just think we both need more time. We need to take things slow to make sure this isn't just trauma bonding or something," Bobbi says.

Julien nods in agreement and squeezes her hands.

Watching them gaze into each other's eyes, I can tell their connection is more than just shared sadness over a lost loved one. Given time, they'll allow themselves to fully give in to the growing feelings they have for each other. With a little more time, they'll let go of the guilt associated with those feelings. And I wish them only the best.

I turn to Art and see he has been watching me. He was clearly concerned that despite what I said before we came here, watching my former best friend and former boyfriend make out on my couch would upset me. I can see how it's a valid deduction to make, but seeing them together actually makes me feel extremely happy and, in a way, at peace. Here are two people I wish I had treated better and appreciated more who have found each other and have the chance to give and receive the kind of deep, devoted love they deserve. A love I wasn't able to provide for them because I lost perspective of what really mattered and became wrapped up completely in my own selfish desires, using them as if they were simply a means to an end and losing my entire sense of self in the process. There's no skirting around that. I mangled my relationship with Bobbi and probably would have with Jules as well if I lived but never came to the realizations I have after death. So, why would I possibly be upset with them for finding happiness within their grief? Truly, I don't know if I could ask for a better outcome.

Art can tell that I'm not upset when he sees the contented smile on my face. His pinched look relaxes, but he still asks me if I'm okay.

"Yes, better than okay really," I assure him. "In fact, right now, I finally feel like I can face the one person I've been avoiding." Although I do mean it, my smile drops at the thought of Dale.

Art doesn't need to ask me who I'm talking about. He reaches out to me and grasps my hand. He asks me, solely through the intensity of his gaze, if I'm sure. I answer without words as well with one quick, decisive nod. He responds by inclining his head towards me and squeezing my hand, as if to say, "Okay, I'm right here with you."

I take comfort from the weight of his hand in mine as I close my eyes and conjure Dale's image. I allow the picture to sit at the front of my mind for three seconds, already having to fend off panic, then open my eyes to face the real thing.

The first thing I notice is the place is a mess. There are dried muddy boot prints weaving a trail around the room along with mud and dirt embedded in the rug lying in front of the discolored couch which may at one point have been green but now has a brown, dusty look. At least a month's worth of newspapers are scattered throughout the space, most of which are torn to pieces and covered in boot prints from being tread on every day. There's also a considerable amount of rat droppings peppering the floor.

We move through the mess and down the hall toward an open room casting a faint light into the hallway. This room isn't much better. Not as many rat droppings, but the bed looks foul. No sheets cover the mattress, so every stain is on full display. A ratty looking blanket crumpled at the foot of the bed fortunately hides at least some of them from view. I try not to think about where those stains may have come from. When I remember how he always left the bar piss drunk, plenty of options present themselves unbidden as explanations for the state of his mattress. Thankfully, the light is fairly dim. The overhead bulb lets off a sickly yellow light. There's also a standing lamp right inside the door with a dying bulb that has a faint orange glow.

My eyes drag themselves to where Dale sits with his back to us at a small desk facing the wall in the far-left corner of the room. He has a small box open in front of him and clutches something from it between his fingers, holding it against his cheek. I see him bring it to his nose to sniff it at least twice.

I approach slowly, picking up and planting my feet down cautiously. The thought occurs to me that the floor wouldn't make a sound even if I stomped over to him, but I keep my slow pace because I'm not all that eager to see what's in the box.

I know I have to look though.

When I come up behind him, I peer over his shoulder, and my

non-existent blood runs cold. There are clippings from the news-papers that all speak of my tragic end and the tireless efforts of the detectives who are working the case night and day. When he moves these aside, I see tons of pictures of me, all candid shots where I am unaware of the photographer. There are photos of me walking down the street, photos of me in my house taken through windows, even photos of me working the bar. Considering the nice photo printer on his desk, the only thing in this house that looks like it gets taken care of, along with the poor quality of some of the pictures, I can only assume he followed me around and took these pictures on his phone to print here.

He would have gotten some suspicious looks if he had tried to get them printed anywhere else.

Even though I dread what I might see, I move to his side to get a look at what he has between his fingers. I stifle my horrified gasp by pressing my hand against my mouth. The clipped section of my hair that the coroner noted missing is threaded between Dale's fin-gers. This is what he has been rubbing against his cheek and sniffing deeply.

Following that shock, I see him pull out one last treasure from his box of secrets, and this is the worst one yet. He places the lock of hair onto the desk in order to fondle the underwear I was wearing that night with both of his hands.

When he lifts these to his nose, panic fills my empty veins causing me to turn and run. All logic is torn from my brain as my neurons are flooded by the belief I am in serious danger. I don't think about ghost traveling far away from here. I don't think about the fact that he can't see me, much less hurt me again.

All I think is: *Run! Get out! Now!*

As I flee the room, I hear the lamp crash to the floor behind me. Then, I hear Dale's booming voice shout, "Hey! Who the fuck is in my house?" His heavy, blundering footsteps follow, and I pick up speed.

I turn the corner heading to the front door just as he storms into the living room. He yells something at the same moment that the door a foot or two in front of me flies open with such force that it slams against the outside wall of the cabin. The loud crash must have made me hear him wrong, because it sounded like he yelled, "I see you!"

The door hangs crooked as it swings back on wobbly hinges. I breeze past it and sprint across a short distance of open field before entering the protective cover of the woods, but Dale is still lumbering after me. I hear him pounding across the yard, screaming, "Get back here, you bitch! Who the fuck are you?"

I don't understand how he can see me, but understanding the situation is not my priority—escape is. I know I'm faster than him, so I keep running. I don't stop until I no longer hear his thundering footsteps.

I stop in a small clearing, bend over slightly with my hands on my thighs, and breathe deeply, not from physical exhaustion, since I don't feel that anymore, but from mental exhaustion. There were so many emotions boiling inside of me in Dale's cabin—anger, disgust, pain, fear. Then the panic sliced through them all and everything turned into chaos in my head.

I try to clear all the emotions away and just breathe, then call for Art. He doesn't appear, but I start to hear Dale's footfalls and heavy breathing again. I scream, "Art! Arthur, please! Where are you?"

Dale crashes into the clearing and stares directly at me. At first, he's all determination and huffing fury, but then he really sees who he's staring at. The realization makes him take a few steps back. His face slackens, mouth opening in shock. He begins shaking his head then whispers, "No, no, no, it can't be you. It just can't. Hannah ... "

I see his terror but don't fully comprehend it because mine is still so fresh. It's pounding in every inch of my body causing me to tremble.

Suddenly, Art is pulling me into an embrace. He's whispering into my ear that it's alright, that he's got me now, that Dale can't hurt me. I cling to him and bury my face into his body. I hear Dale shuffling around and, with real panic in his voice, asking, "Hannah? Hannah? Where'd you go? Where are you? Please, Hannah. I'm sorry. I'm sorry!" I hear him fleeing. Still, I don't look. I stay in the protective circle of Art's arms and keep my face pressed to his chest, focusing on the rise and fall of his breath.

Finally, when all is quiet, I turn my head so Art can hear me and say, "Take me somewhere, Art. I don't care where. Just take me away from here, okay? I want to be far, far away from here. Please."

He wraps his arms tighter around me and begins to stroke my hair. He whispers back, "Of course, Hannah. Just close your eyes and breathe. I've got you. You're okay."

I stand intertwined with Art for several moments, eyes closed and matching my breathing to his, and he lets me. He doesn't unfurl his arms from around me or tell me we've made it to wherever he's taken me. He continues to hold me until that faint flicker of warmth sputters to life in my stomach. Every time it's happened before now, I got excited and felt hopeful. This time, it just feels like yet another thing I don't understand, so I pull away from him and let the sensation fade away.

I take a look around to see where he's brought me. What I see is a pristine, peaceful lake overlooked by mountains far in the distance. Behind me is a pleasant-looking cabin with a couple of rocking chairs and a long swing on the porch looking out at the lake. The grass is overgrown and weeds have begun snaking up the building, but it still holds a warm, welcoming feel, as if all the love this cabin has seen and held inside it has burrowed into its foundation. The snow falling and settling over the scene just adds to the soft, gentle feel of the place.

I try to picture it as Art had described it to me before. I conjure up two loving parents dancing in the kitchen. I see the kids rolling their eyes and finishing their meal quickly so they can race down the steps to the lake. The parents stroll onto the porch after them with lazy smiles born from peaceful vacationing. They sit in the rocking chairs and keep their hands held loosely together, languidly brushing their thumbs along the back of the other's hand as they watch their children with amusement sparkling in their eyes.

I look to the lake and try to imagine a young Art splashing around without a single care in the world and no concerns about the future. I try to picture his face without the sharpness I'm used to but instead rounded out with baby fat. His smile still uniquely his, as it always will be. A smile I'm positive I could identify among any number of others at a single glance.

"Are you okay now, Hannah?" Art's question brings me out of my reverie.

"Yeah, and thank you," I reply and nod toward the porch.

Art and I head up the steps, and he follows me to the porch swing. We sit silently for a few moments—me enjoying the view, Art most likely lost in memories. I don't interrupt his reminiscence. I gaze across the lake and wait.

"I've missed this place," Art breaks the silence.

"When was the last time you came here?" I ask.

"We only came as a family once after my dad died. After that, my mom let my siblings use it for their families. Once, a few months after I died, I was feeling really lonely and decided to go see one of my brothers. I ended up here. He was in the lake with his little girl and his wife. It was just too much for me. I wasn't upset with him for coming here and trying to have a good time with his family. It was just being here again. There were too many memories."

"And now?" I ask.

"I think telling you about it helped. Telling you about my parents, about my dad," he answers, and I'm so tempted to tell him it would probably help him to talk about his mom too. I don't though. This is not something I want to force out of him.

"It's a beautiful place, so serene," I say instead.

"It was the first place that came to mind when you asked me to take you away. It's far away and peaceful. Seemed fitting," Art replies and finally relaxes his posture, leaning back against the swing and turning his head to look at me.

"Thank you, Art. I'm really glad you were there," I say and reach out to give his hand a quick squeeze.

As I'm withdrawing my hand, he takes it in one of his. He holds our hands between us and gazes down at them for several moments before unfurling his fingers. I slowly bring my hand back down to my lap and try to discern from Art's face what it is he's thinking, but mind reading is not a specialty of mine. Instead, I rest my head against his shoulder and match my breathing to his again.

After a few moments of silence, I get an idea and ask, "Would you sing me another song?"

Art chuckles and answers, "If you really want me to, I guess. Give me a minute to think of a good one."

"Do you know any Columbian songs?" I ask, and hold my breath.

I feel his muscles tense and his breath hitch slightly. He's silent for a few moments before answering, "Only a lullaby."

"Can you sing that for me?" I ask. Then, after a long silence, I add, "Please?"

"Alright, but only if you dance with me," Art says.

I sit up straight and look at him quizzically. He looks back at me with a grin tugging at the corner of his lips. He's still a bit stiff, but there's a playfulness to him so I must not have upset him too badly.

"Dance to a lullaby?" I ask, as if the logistics of the idea are impossible.

"That's the deal. Take it or leave it," Art replies, then stands and holds his hand out to me with a slight bow.

I let out an amused chuckle and take his hand. He pulls me up, wraps an arm around my waist, and keeping my hand in his begins to sway. We stay like this, moving like trees in a soft breeze, for a few silent moments before he begins to sing.

Arrorró mi niño,
arrorró mi sol,
arrorró pedazo
de mi corazón.
Este niño lindo
se quiere dormir
y el pícaro sueño
no quiere venir.

He sings the whole lullaby as we dance in a small circle. I rest my head against his chest again, and he rests his head on mine. My cheek pressed against his chest begins to feel as if it is thawing but, before it starts to feel warm, the song ends. Art takes a step back and twirls me once before letting my hand fall from his.

After a few beats of silence where we just stare at each other, I ask, "How were you able to remember the whole thing?"

"She used to sing it to us when we felt really sick, no matter how old we were. I probably got some of it wrong though," Art replies.

"Did she sing it to you in the hospital?" I ask and immediately regret it when I see his face fall into a pained grimace.

"Once, before she left in tears and didn't come back unless the doctors needed her for something," Art replies.

"Art, I'm so sorry," I say, unsure what words could erase what I just brought up for him. Except, he doesn't need it erased. That's the whole reason we're stuck here, because we have been hiding from the things we don't want to face. The only difference between us is I was hiding in life, and he's hiding in death.

I continue, "That must have been incredibly difficult for you, and I'm so sorry you had to go through that alone. But don't you think that perhaps she—"

"I don't want to talk about this anymore. Okay, Hannah?" Art asks. He holds his hands as fists at his sides to control their trembling.

"Okay," I agree in concern and lift both of his hands. At my touch, he lets them unclench, and I sandwich his hands between mine. "Just remember what I told you, Art. I'm not going to leave you behind."

"What if they catch Dale and you see your light because there's nothing more for you here but I still don't see mine?" Art asks.

"I won't go," I reply, and I've never meant anything that I've said more than this simple statement.

"You may not be able to resist it," Art says, refusing to look at me.

I cup his chin in my hand and turn his face towards mine. My gaze is steady, unblinking, maybe intense, but Art holds it. I see the pain and uncertainty in his eyes which makes mine ache for tears that won't come.

"I'm not going anywhere without you, Arthur," I say.

He looks steadily into my eyes for a few moments, then he leans forward and places his forehead against mine. We stand like this as the seconds tick by with my heart doing acrobatics in my chest. When he finally speaks, I don't register his words at first, only his breath caressing my skin.

"Thank you, Hannah," is what he says.

Only because I can think of no other response, I reply, "You're welcome."

I don't think I've fully convinced him I would be able to resist entering my light if I were to see mine first, but he seems to have taken comfort in the fact that I mean what I've said in this moment. Perhaps the present is the most important thing. Being here with Art, far from all the mess at home, simply enjoying these moments with him, becoming closer to him, seems like the only thing that matters.

It *is* the only thing that matters, because it's right here in front of me. I've let too many things go from focusing too intently on the bigger picture. Right now, I want to focus on this one snapshot in time, because I know it's a picture worth framing.

We stay at the house all night, joking and laughing under the stars or sitting quietly to listen to the life of the lake. Frogs croak. Crickets sing. Owls hoot. Leaves rustle. And the surface of the water whispers with the wind.

We are sitting on the porch steps when morning comes, and we watch the lake turn golden as the sun rises behind it. Art's hand rests familiarly on my knee, as if that's the most natural place for it to be. I still feel cold, but the chill doesn't feel bone deep anymore. I breathe in the fresh morning air, the scent of winter floating gently in the breeze, and feel at ease.

I put a plea out into the universe for whoever is in charge. No matter what awaits me after my business here is done, please let me hold on to this moment. I don't ever want to forget the beauty around me and the peace inside of me. Let me keep this.

15

When I decide it's time to go back, our first stop is my mom's house. I was planning to check on her then go see the detectives, but they are at the house talking to my mother when we get there.

"We've been testing the blood samples we took for any kind of drug that could be used to knock a person out, but we weren't getting any hits. After we spoke to you, I asked them to check for animal tranquilizers since you mentioned he has a small farm. We got results in today with a match for a horse tranquilizer," Winslow is telling my mom.

"That bastard," she manages to hiss out between clenched teeth. Her hands are also clenched, and Winslow places one of his over hers.

"I know it's hard to hear, but this is a good lead," Winslow says. "We've spoken to the owner of the farming supply store. He happens to be a licensed veterinarian too, so he can sell those type of medicines. We've got a list of everyone who bought the tranquilizer from the past three months."

"Is Dale on it?" my mom asks.

"He is. Twice, in fact," Dennis answers. "The owner pointed it out to us when we asked him if he ever got an odd feeling about a sale or if he ever felt suspicious in any way about a customer. He said Dale is a regular at his store, very interested in fully immersing himself in the farming lifestyle. The guy said he showed Dale a couple years ago how to give his animals injections because Dale asked, saying he wanted to be the one to do all the caretaking of his animals. The owner said Dale purchased the tranquilizer in September, then came back the next month for more. He said that's fairly odd since not enough time had passed for him to use all that tranquilizer, but he didn't question him too much because Dale never gave him any trouble before. He did say he was going to question him further if he came in again asking for more."

"Do you think this is enough to get him?" my mom asks.

"It's enough for a warrant," Winslow assures her. "We're going to take another trip over to his cabin first. I'm going to lay it all out and tell him it's in his best interest to give a DNA sample over willingly. If he still refuses, we'll immediately start the process for a warrant."

"He'll never cooperate, not unless you make him," my mom says.

"Probably true, but he also may panic and say too much once we question him about something solid like these tranquilizers. Panic is the downfall of most criminals. If he slips up on any detail, no matter how small, that will be another point against him, another reason for suspicion. We can use as many as we can get," Dennis explains.

My mom examines both detectives, looks into their eyes, and sees their confidence is genuine. She relaxes into the couch and nods slowly. She's starting to get the faraway look in her eyes.

"Ms. King? Are you all right?" Winslow asks.

My mom gives her head a small shake and focuses on him again. "Yes, I'm sorry," she mutters. "Just a lot on my mind."

"Of course, ma'am. We should get going. You take it easy, okay? We're very close now," Winslow says.

"Thank you," my mom replies, standing as they do and moving towards the door. "I hope you know how much I appreciate you both keeping me updated."

"I wouldn't think to do it any other way, ma'am," Winslow replies and takes her hand. "It's a tough enough situation as it is without having to sit around wondering what's going on or feeling like you need to hound us for information. After myself and Dennis, you should be the first to hear of every development in this case. I never want you to feel like you are in the dark."

"And I haven't, not even for a moment," my mom assures him and graces him with a genuine smile. Since it has become so rare for me to see my mom smile of late, I want to hug Winslow for drawing one out of her.

"Well then, I guess I'm doing my job right," he says and returns her smile. "Now, we'd better get moving. It's past time we go out there and finish this. It won't be long now, ma'am."

"Thank you, John. You too, Dennis," my mom calls to them as they head down the driveway toward their car. They wave goodbye as they get in, and she waves back before shutting the door.

I really want to follow Winslow and Dennis to see how their talk with Dale pans out, but the memory of running from Dale and feeling his eyes on me again is still so fresh. I'm afraid to see him again, afraid he will see *me* again.

Art must have seen the anxiety in my face because he offers, "I could go on my own if you need me to."

I shake my head and reply, "I should be there. I want to be there. I want to see him sweat. It's just that things seem a lot more complicated now."

"Hey, think about it this way. If he does see you while the detectives are there, they could probably grab him right then and lock him up in a mental institution," Art jokes.

"Maybe, but that's not where I want to see him locked up," I reply.

Art nods and replies, "The offer to go on my own still stands, but I really don't think he'll be able to see you again. Last time, we didn't know what to expect. What you saw was extremely disturbing, so obviously your emotional response was off the charts. We've already theorized that harnessing your strong emotions can help you pull back the curtain, so to speak. You were in a panic, so how your energy interacted with the world around you was unpredictable and ended up pulling the curtain back a lot further than you've been able to before. This time, we have a better idea of what we'll see. The detectives will be questioning him, putting pressure on him, and it may shake him up. I think it's more likely he will be the one experiencing out-of-control emotions instead of you."

Like everything else Art says, it makes sense. I start to feel more confident about going back. Plus, if Dale does end up panicking and making a fool of himself, I desperately want to be there to see it happen.

"Alright," I say with a firm nod of my head and reach my hand out to Art. "Let's do it." He takes my hand and gives it an encouraging squeeze as we close our eyes.

I picture Dale's cabin instead of his face, so we are standing a few feet away from the porch steps when we open our eyes. The detectives' car is nowhere in sight, which is why I'm glad we are not inside with Dale just yet, so we wait on the porch until they arrive.

We don't have to wait long, as they pull in about five minutes after we show up. Winslow heads directly to the front door while Dennis walks around to the side of the house as nonchalantly as he can to get a view of the small pen of animals situated in the back. A moderately sized barn is connected to the pen so the animals can go in and out as they please. He sees a cow lazily gnawing on grass, a pig basking in the sun, a few chickens bobbing their heads as they skitter around, and a horse happily trotting around after a small goat that is bouncing around, kicking itself off of haybales and the chicken coop. He has time to take in the scene then shamble back to the front of the house to join Winslow before Dale responds to the persistent knocking at his door.

Dale's face already looks pale and gaunt when he opens the door, but it loses even more color when he registers who is on his porch.

"Do you remember us, Mr. Evans? We came by once before asking for a DNA sample," Winslow begins.

"Yeah," Dale answers. He tries to force a smile but it trembles. "Sorry, but my answer would still be no if you've come to ask again. I just don't feel comfortable with it. I didn't do nothing, so I don't see a reason for it to be necessary."

"We would, of course, respect that decision," Winslow replies with the utmost professionalism. "However, some new evidence has presented itself, and I think it would be in your best interest to hear us out. May we come in?"

Dale's lips begin to twitch, which he tries to hide with another shaky smile.

"The place ain't too clean," he says.

"Oh, we've seen everything there is to see, sir. I doubt if any mess in there will bother us any," Winslow replies.

Dale reluctantly lets them in then shuffles ahead of them into the disastrous living room. Winslow diplomatically does not comment on the mess or even scrutinize it for more than a second. Dennis, on the other hand, takes a look around and points out the mice droppings.

"You should get a cat, Mr. Evans. Lots of farms keep at least one cat around to control the mice," he says in a friendly manner. It's the first time I've seen him hold back what he's actually feeling and act the complete opposite, and surprisingly convincing.

Dale takes a look around the room as if he's never noticed the droppings before and replies, "Yeah, I 'spose you're right about that." Then he offers the detectives the only seat in the room, motioning toward the couch.

There's a brief moment of silence as Winslow and Dennis glance at each other, then at the couch.

"That's a kind offer, but we want you to feel comfortable. You can take the couch. We can get a couple of chairs from the kitchen, if you'd be alright with that," Winslow says.

"Sure, however you wanna do it," Dale grunts, and the couch squeals when he places his weight on it.

Once the chairs are set up and, with a surprising agreement from Dale, his tape recorder is rolling, Winslow begins, "Mr. Evans, we wanted to speak to you about your recent purchases from the farming supply store you frequent. In particular, we are curious about the two vials of horse tranquilizers you purchased just a month apart from each other. Mr. Williams at the supply store seemed to think that was odd considering the vials have multiple doses, especially considering the reason you gave him when you bought the first vial was that your horse is extremely temperamental and had gotten into the habit of not allowing you to trim his hooves. You said you needed small doses to calm him down in order to take care of him, isn't that right?"

"Well, yeah, sure," Dale answers. "I don't see what this got to do with anything though. I lost the first vial and needed another. Why are you interested to begin with?"

"Because that same tranquilizer was used to debilitate Hannah the night she was killed," Dennis says. The nice guy act forgotten.

Color returns to Dale's cheeks as his face flushes, and he replies,

"And just because I bought it, you think I'm the one who did it?"

"We received a list of people who ordered that tranquilizer, and it didn't have very many names on it. Your name was on there twice, and you refuse to give us a DNA sample. It raises some questions, that's all we're saying," Dennis answers as he stares steadily at Dale.

Dale tries to hold the gaze, but his eyes keep darting down to his feet or around the room. When Dennis finishes speaking, Dale gets to his feet and points a dirty, pudgy finger in his direction.

"That is not all you're saying, not one bit!" he yells ,then begins to pace around the room, kicking at scraps of old newspaper. "You assholes don't have a single lead, so you just wanna pin it on the first guy you can. Well, I ain't gonna let ya! You think I could'a done that to that poor, sweet child? She was a peach, an angel! What kinda man could see that beauty and smash it to pieces? Then left her out there all exposed to the elements, even took her fuckin' underwear! You tell me if you can, what kinda man could do that?"

At the mention of the stolen underwear, Dennis and Winslow sneak a glance at each other. I can see the excitement flare in their eyes, like a hunter seeing an animal caught in his trap ... because this was a detail that was never released to the public.

Dale realizes his mistake and stops mid-stride. He hurriedly conjures up an explanation, stating, "Of course, that's just a rumor I heard at Jimmy's. May not be more than some drunks talking outta their asses." He glances at the tape recorder, sweat beading on his forehead.

"Jimmy's, that's the bar Hannah worked at, correct?" Winslow asks as he jots a note down on his notepad.

Dale looks nervously at the notepad. His tongue darts out to wet his lips.

"Well, it ain't just a bar. Pretty damn good restaurant," Dale tries to answer casually but there is a tremor in his voice and his breathing has become quick and shallow.

"Mr. Evans, if you're innocent, you have nothing to worry about," Winslow says. "Providing us with a DNA sample would do nothing except remove your name from our list, and we could all move on. If you refuse again, we'll be forced to move forward with a warrant."

"I know I'm innocent," Dale replies unsteadily. "All you've got is a couple'a lousy receipts."

"Okay, Mr. Evans. Have it your way," Winslow says with a smile. He packs his things back into his briefcase, then he and Dennis show themselves to the door.

"This door looks like it needs to be adjusted. Something happen?" Dennis asks as he steps out onto the porch.

"Ain't none'a your business," Dale replies and wrestles the door back into its jamb.

He watches as the detectives get in their car and drive away. When he can no longer see their vehicle he hurries to the bedroom and grabs the box from his wardrobe. He opens it and takes a lighter from his pocket, which he ignites. He holds the lighter over the box with one hand and gently touches the snapshots of me with the other. With a pained groan, he extinguishes the lighter and shoves the box under his arm.

Art and I follow him to the barn and watch as he brings the box up into the hayloft. He sits against bales of hay with the box in his lap. He's clearly obsessed with the contents, but they also haunt him. For both of these reasons he can't bring himself to destroy it.

He begins to cry, and it is music to my ears. A sociopathic grin tugs at my lips as I listen. I know I have a very good excuse, but I can't help but feel deep down that experiencing so much happiness from someone else's pain makes me a bit crazy.

I don't have to dwell on that thought for long though because a familiar tugging in my gut tells me it's time to leave.

I reach my hand out to Art, and he takes it without question.

I close my eyes and, when I no longer hear Dale's sobs, open them to the sight of my grave.

I didn't actually look at it at the funeral. The engraving reads "Hannah King, June 22, 1997 – November 13, 2019, Beloved daughter." I move my eyes further down and notice grass peeking out of the snow, grass that has sprouted from the dirt above my body.

Nature carries on.

Approaching footsteps distract me from that particular line of thinking, and I brighten when I see Bobbi heading in my direction. My smile falters when I see how upset she looks. Her mouth is turned down at the corners, a gesture I know means she's thinking of something unpleasant, and her hands twist the ends of her scarf. When she reaches the gravestone, she sits cross-legged on the ground near it and places her hand on its side.

"Hannah," she whispers. Despite the years spent apart, I can detect her emotions better than I can detect my own. There's worry and guilt in the tremor of her voice, and I know what's on her mind before she continues. "That night at the bar, I could see that you felt guilty when you lied about not having an extra towel for me to use after Christine poured her drink on me. Now it's my turn to feel guilty, and I think what I've done is much worse. I have a strong feeling that you're still around so maybe you already know, though I would have expected a reaction similar to what happened at the funeral home if you did. Even if you do already know, I need to say it. Julien and I have been spending a lot of time together. Last night, things got emotional. We ended up kissing. It all happened so fast, but I did want it. I still do. God, I'm the worst friend ever."

I look around for anything I could use to send her a message—a truce offering. My eyes lock on the apple tree. I couldn't do anything to it the last time I was here with my mom, but since then I apparently threw Dale's door open without even touching it.

I should be able to pick a damn apple.

I stand beside the tree and close my eyes, listening to Bobbi pour her heart out, letting her emotions and mine mingle together in my heart.

"We agreed to take things very slow. We want to be sure these feelings are real and not born from our grief, because we are still grieving. I know after what I just told you it may not seem like we are, but it's true. I think it is real though, how we feel about each other. It's much more genuine than what I felt with Mark. I just wish I knew whether you were okay with it or not. I told him you'd want us to be happy and continue on with our lives, but I'm afraid of taking that too far. What I really want you to know is that we both still love you so much, and nothing will ever change that."

She's standing now, turning my way to head back to the gate. It's now or never. I don't let any doubts or thoughts enter my head. I hold on to the feelings Bobbi poured out, letting them nourish me and give me the strength I need. Just as she turns toward the path, with the apple tree directly in her line of vision, I quickly reach out and snatch an apple off its branch.

Bobbi hears the snap and sees an apple hovering disconnected as I walk forward a few steps. She calls my name hesitantly, and in her eyes I see she thinks the apple may come hurtling toward her head at any second. I squat down, planning to roll it to her, but it passes through my hand and drops to the ground. I curse and try to focus again.

Bobbi shakes off her uncertainty and walks toward the fallen apple. When she has halved the distance between us, I take a deep breath and push the apple forward. It rolls the rest of the distance and bumps against Bobbi's shoe. Gingerly she reaches down and picks it up. Cradling the apple in her hands, she holds it against her chest and scans the area around the tree. She holds it tight, squeezing it rhythmically like a stress ball.

"Thank you, Hannah. I miss you so much. I hope you get to rest peacefully soon. They'll get him. I know they will," she says.

"I miss you too," I whisper to her back as she walks down the path to the gate. Then I go back to the gravestone where Art has been standing and watching.

"Yet another miracle," Art says only halfway joking. I can see in his eyes that he does believe the things I can do are miraculous, even if it's simply picking an apple and holding it for a few seconds. "You're full of them! Is it getting easier to control?"

"Please don't call them miracles," I mumble and roll my eyes. "Anomaly is probably more accurate. But yes, I think it is getting easier. At least to turn it on. I still can't seem to keep hold of something for longer than a few seconds."

"I've got a feeling that's not why you look so bummed right now," Art replies.

I had averted my eyes to the ground, but now I look up into his expectant and reassuring gaze. The warmth of his eyes calling to me like gentle birdsong on a summer morning.

"I'm just blown away at how loyal she continues to be to our friendship even after all I did to her," I explain. "The fact she defended me when Winslow brought up the bullying that Christine and Shelley mentioned, she was there for me that night at the bar, she came to my service and held my mom when I couldn't, and she feels the need to apologize to *me* for finding some happiness amidst all this sadness. As if I would tell them they aren't allowed to have any joy now that I'm gone, and she'd actually consider giving it up. How can she still care so much about my approval after everything I put her through?"

"Hannah, she could see that the person who was teasing her was never who you really were deep down, and she forgave you for it. So, why can't you?" Art asks, then pauses and studies my face. He looks deeper into my eyes, into my soul—more so than anyone ever has. He sees the real me, and I can almost see that person reflected back to me. A knot forms in my throat as he continues, "And I can see that you were never that person. You were able to shut your emotions off to act cold towards her, but now …"

"Now, what?" I ask, feeling breathless from his unwavering eye contact.

"Now, I think you know the act was never necessary. You never needed to hide your emotions, and you especially don't need to hide them here. Because here, it's just you and me. And I always want you to be who you truly are."

He cups my cheek in his hand, and it feels as if he's placed a small heating pack against my skin. That feeling of a slow, budding warmth I've gotten several times when he's touched me has upgraded to a steady heat. I rub my cheek against his palm, savoring the feel of his warm skin thawing mine just like his words melted the last bits of frost from my heart.

I reach up with my hand and cup his cheek too. A short breath of shock escapes his lips at my touch. He keeps the hand on my cheek where it is and, with his other hand, reaches up and covers mine that is cradling his face. Our eyes meet, and an understanding passes between us. An understanding there must be a reason this warmth has bloomed, but it's better to simply enjoy it rather than try to analyze it, at least for the moment. I tug on his shirt to pull him towards me. His arms wrap around my waist and mine around his neck. I stand on my tiptoes in order to rest my head on his shoulder.

The persistent chill that has clung to me ever since waking up here rapidly dissipates. Art's warmth envelopes me completely and begins to seep into me. I lower myself from my tiptoe position and nestle my face against his chest wanting more, and never wanting the warmth to go away.

16

The heat gradually dims until it feels more like the budding warmth I've felt before. We don't want to let go of each other, afraid that breaking contact would bring back the chill and completely smother the lingering warmth, so we keep our hands clasped as we walk to my mom's house.

"I've felt these flickers of warmth when we've touched several times before. It started out as just a hint, barely noticeable, but gradually became like a flickering flame. Did you ever notice anything like that?" I ask, finally feeling confident enough to do so since I know for certain he did at least feel it this time.

"Exactly the same," Art replies, sounding relieved. "I never said anything because I wasn't sure that you felt it. Even if you did, I thought you might ask me to explain, and I have no clue what it means."

Except, I think we both know what it means, but we can't say it out loud because it would complicate things. Admitting our growing feelings for each other would make it so much harder to leave when the time comes. Neither one of us wants to be stuck in this limbo state forever, even if it meant we could be together.

"Maybe we should let go," I say and lift our interlocked hands.

Art stops walking and asks, "Why?"

I hear the disappointment in his voice. He tightens his grip slightly and brings our combined hands towards his chest. His eyes call to me, and as I stare into them, I want to tell him I never want him to let go of me.

Instead I explain, "I just think we should see what happens if we let go. I know the feeling went away when we stopped touching the other times, but this time felt a lot different. I'm curious to know if it'll last this time."

Art stares down at our hands, his thumb brushing back and forth against my skin. As I watch his contemplative face and his expressive eyes, it becomes clear to me there's more to his reluctance than not wanting the warmth to go away.

"Art?" I say softly to get his attention. When he focuses his eyes back to mine, I continue, "You don't have to let go forever. My hand will still be here, you know?"

Immediately after the words leave my mouth, I feel pathetic and awkward. There had to have been a better way to say that. It's like I forgot how to talk to a boy. I'm about to avert my eyes in shame but, before I can, the sweetest smile I've ever seen spreads across Art's face, and it's like I can see joy dancing amongst the forest that is his eyes.

"Well, alright then," he replies timidly. He gives my hand a final squeeze before letting it go. He keeps eye contact with me, and his smile softens as the moments tick by.

Staring into his eyes is like a meditation. I always feel calm when I gaze into his shining brown eyes and lose myself among the specks of green.

"I still feel it," I say after an acceptable amount of time passes.

"I do too," Art replies, still grinning.

"This is good! We're discovering things. Learning, in a way," I reply, and now I can't keep a smile off of my face. A smile born from equal parts nerves and excitement.

Art lets out a sigh, but he's still content enough to where it doesn't sound overly upset, and says, "Sadly, discovery doesn't always lead to understanding. There is still a lot we don't understand about our situation."

"And still so much to do," I add. "We should just focus on moving forward."

Art nods his head in agreement, but there is a hint of disappointment in his eyes and his words as he looks up and he says, "Yeah, we should keep going."

As we continue our walk, I keep looking down at Art's hand, willing it to reach out to mine again, but he doesn't try to hold my hand the rest of the way to my mom's house. We walk in silence, both of us lost in our own thoughts. Mine revolving mostly around him. I wish I knew what was going on in his head. Is he thinking of me? And if he is, is he focusing on our seemingly growing attraction to each other, or is he worrying about losing me? I saw that worry in his eyes at the cabin when he asked me what would happen if I saw my light before he did. I want to search his eyes for it now, but his head is angled down. His hair hides his eyes from me along with most of his face. I'm about to overcome my doubt and reach out and slip my hand back into his when he suddenly stops and looks back to me.

"Here we are," he says before disappearing through the front door of my mom's house. I was completely focused on my internal debate I wasn't even paying attention to where I was walking. I quickly follow Art into the house and am greeted by a delicious assortment of smells.

"Just in time for dinner," I say to Art as we let our noses carry us to the kitchen.

My mom is bustling around the room when we enter. She sets three spots at the table and takes a moment between each to stir the sides of corn and green beans heating on the stove. Once the places are set, she takes a pan out of the oven with three baked potatoes wrapped in foil on it. The smell of the pork roast fills the room as she gives it a short inspection before closing the oven to let it cook a few minutes longer.

The doorbell rings, and my mom hurries to answer it. Bobbi is waiting patiently on the other side. When it opens, she gives my mom a bright smile and a tight hug. My mom ushers her in and asks, "Where's Jean?"

"Mom isn't feeling too good this evening," Bobbi answers. "She said to tell you she's real sorry but she didn't want to risk getting you sick."

"Oh, I'm sorry to hear that. You tell her not to worry about it though, and you can take some for her when you leave. I'm glad you still came," my mom says and pats Bobbi's cheek.

"Of course, I wouldn't want to miss it. It smells amazing. Is there anything I can help with?" Bobbi asks.

"No, no, I just need to take the roast out, then you can fill up your plate," my mom answers as she slips on her oven mitts.

She deems the roast tender enough, so they both pile food onto their plates and take their seats at the table. The conversation between and around bites of food mostly has to do with Bobbi's classes and what plans she has for winter break. It's just small talk about everyday things, but it's heartwarming to know that my mom can have still have these simple moments with Bobbi even if she can no longer have them with me. I see it in her eyes occasionally throughout the conversation—that pained, glazed look. But it seems like she's finding it easier to keep the dark thoughts at bay.

With the meal finished, Bobbi and my mom move to the living room to lounge on the couch. Bobbi takes a deep breath before changing the tone of the conversation by saying, "I'm sort of glad my mom isn't here because there's something I'd really like to talk to you about."

My mom looks intrigued and encourages her to go on, so she starts by explaining the night her and Julien kissed. Mom, thinking this was the big thing Bobbi wanted to talk about, says, "Sweetheart, you don't need to worry yourself sick over falling for him. It's not a betrayal, and it does not make you a bad friend. I think Hannah would love the idea actually. She'd be happy that you two find comfort in each other and could possibly find healing there too."

"Yeah, I think you're right. That's what I really want to talk to you about. I went to the cemetery to talk to her, to confess really. I felt so horrible, but then something amazing happened." Bobbi reaches into the pocket of her sweatpants and brings out an apple. "This apple snapped off the branch and hovered in the air for a few moments before it fell to the ground. I went to go pick it up, and it rolled directly to me, stopping right at my feet."

My mom is sitting with her hands in a temple shape in front of her face covering her mouth and nose. After Bobbi finishes her story, my mom moves her hands to her heart and reveals a beaming smile on her face.

"You see? We were right," my mom says. "She is still here. Remember back when my sister was visiting? You and your mom came and ate burgers with us. When we were talking, I felt a breath against my neck. It was exactly what Hannah used to do to scare me."

"She must still be here for a reason though. I wish I could do something for her," Bobbi says as she absent-mindedly turns the apple over and over in her hands.

"I think she just needs to see Dale gets what he deserves," my mom says. "The detectives think they're close. I sure hope they're right."

My mom's phone starts emitting her obnoxiously loud ringtone causing them both to jolt out of their silent musings. She grabs the phone and tells Bobbi that it's Julien calling before she answers it.

"Hi Julien, how are you?" she asks.

There's silence in the room as Julien talks on the other end of the call.

"Did you call Winslow?"

Another short pause.

"Good. I'm on my way," my mom says before shutting her phone off. Then she's up on her feet and dashing for her keys.

"What is it?" Bobbi asks as she heads to the door.

"Julien found a camera hidden on the shelf where Hannah kept all the little figurine statues she collected from thrift stores. He said Winslow was already on the way," my mom explains as they hustle into the car.

I hesitate for only a second before passing through the door and sliding into the backseat, getting in the same way I would if the door wasn't closed. I scoot all the way over to make room as Art follows right behind me. He makes it just in time as my mom slams the car into gear and speeds off.

Everyone in the car is silent as nervous anticipation fills the air. My mom grips the steering wheel so hard it seems like her knuckles may tear open her skin. Bobbi still holds the apple tightly in her grip as she mindlessly leaves little crescent moon shapes in the apple's skin with her fingernails. Art is drumming his fingers on the door under the window as he gazes out at the passing scenery. He looks over at me, and I see nervousness in his expression but also a sort of wonder.

"I never tried this since becoming a ghost, or whatever we are. Riding in a car with somebody. It's sort of weird how such a mundane thing can be so fascinating to me now," Art says.

"Well, it has been a lot longer since you've been in a car, but I did hesitate for a second before getting in. I wasn't sure it would work. Of course, if it hadn't, we could've just used our regular form of travel," I say, and my hand itches to reach out to hold his at the thought of how we have been traveling hand-in-hand everywhere we go.

Maybe he had the same thought, or maybe it was just the sight of my hand resting on the seat between us, but his hand inches its way along the seat until it covers mine. His pinkie begins lightly brushing back and forth across my thumb. I watch with a grin creeping onto my face.

He stops along with the car as my mom parks next to Julien's motorcycle in the driveway. We all get out, and I see the detectives' car parked alongside the road by the mailbox.

Inside, Winslow is on the phone asking about the possibility of obtaining Dale's recent credit card bills once the warrant is processed. He acknowledges my mom, giving her arm a light squeeze, then motions them back toward the bedroom where Dennis and Julien are. Dennis is listening intently to Julien explaining how he found the camera.

"I was boxing up some of Hannah's things that I thought Ms. Carolyn might like to have," he looks at my mom as he says this, and she gives him a small smile with tears clinging to her eyelashes.

He continues, "It was nestled behind a group of her little statues. I picked it up to take it off the shelf and noticed the cord that goes through the shelf here. I mean, he must have had to pull the shelf forward a bit, drill a hole in it, run the cord through and plug it in to the outlet behind there. He couldn't have possibly known about that outlet though! It makes no sense! How can this asshole be so meticulous but also seem like he was just winging it? How could he get so goddamn lucky?"

Julien's voice rises as he speaks until he screams the last question. He punctuates the word "lucky" by smacking the lamp off the bedside table in frustration.

Bobbi doesn't hesitate to go to him. She takes his shaking hands in hers and squeezes them as she brings them to her lips. He looks into her eyes to steady himself and takes a deep breath which he lets out shakily, but his hands are no longer trembling.

"He won't be lucky for much longer, if he ever was to begin with," Dennis assures Julien as he steps out the room to find Winslow.

The room is quiet as they wait. My mom starts going through the box of my thrift store finds while Bobbi and Julien stand holding each other. A weighty anticipation hangs in the air between us all. The pieces of this puzzle are finally coming together, and it feels like they are snowballing towards a conclusion. I get a strong feeling this is the most important piece. The one that will bring the whole world crumbling down around Dale.

When Winslow returns with Dennis, everyone's attention focuses on him. It's been clear to me from the beginning what a commanding presence Winslow has, like a sage everyone looks to for understanding. When he's around, you're drawn to him. You want to tell him all your worries because you somehow know he will have an answer for you. Even if he can't give you a clear-cut solution, he will have beneficial wisdom to impart to you that could lead you to your own answer. So, naturally, everyone looks to him when they want to know what comes next. He looks unwaveringly into each of their searching eyes. They see strength and determination in that gaze, and they begin to build their own confidence on the foundation of his. The anticipation begins to lift off their shoulders as they sense the wait is finally over. Something big is about to happen. Everyone can feel it.

Pointing to where the cord still pokes out from the drilled hole in the back of the shelf, Winslow says, "Because this camera was plugged in, we can assume it was able to record continuously. He may have still been watching even after all these weeks. If he was, then Mr. Stoll finding it and us disabling it has tipped him off. Dennis and I are going to go pay Dale another visit as soon as the officers I called to collect the camera for evidence show up. One of them will stay here with the three of you. I think it's wise to stay together for now until we ascertain if he is currently a threat. Acceptable arrangement?"

Everyone nods in response.

The sound of people entering the house drifts down the hall. Winslow claps his hands and mutters "Excellent" as he hurries down the hall to meet the other officers.

"Come on," I say to Art as I grab his hand and lead him out of the house. "We're going with Winslow and Dennis."

Art gives my hand a supportive squeeze, letting me know he's with me using touch instead of words. I feel like I'm getting good at reading him, whether it's through body language, picking up subtleties in his voice, or seeing hidden emotions in his eyes. I cling tighter to his hand as the thought that my story may be coming to an end soon rises in my mind like a menacing tidal wave. I also hold tight to the promise I made that I will not leave without him. I'm determined to keep eternity at bay until I can go into it with Art by my side.

We slip into the backseat of the detectives' cruiser as they are exiting the house. Art hasn't let go of me and is moving his thumb in calming circles on the back of my hand. He keeps the same pace during the entire ride. I'm still deep in thought, and I'm sure he is as well, but I think the physical connection helps to keep us from getting lost in contemplation.

When the car stops in front of Dale's cabin, we hesitantly let go of each other's hand and follow the detectives up to the front door. Neither of them knocks. They stand for a moment staring at the door, then curses fly from their mouths as they hurry back to the car.

As they retreat, I see what they were staring at. There is a note nailed to the door. I stand in front of it and read as they speed away in the car.

The note reads:

To whoever comes looking for me,

I can't do it anymore. I probably could have made a good defense case if it were just the two bottles of tranq and the camera. Circumstantial I think is what they call it. Probably not strong enough to put me in jail. But they'll get my DNA. And then I won't be able to hide from the truth anymore. It's been getting harder to live with anyway.

So I've gone to join her in the place I lost her. God forgive me.

"He's going to kill himself," I mutter hopelessly. The idea that he will take the easy way out in order to avoid punishment, that he may have already done it, should make me angry. I want to be angry. But all of my energy drains out of me after reading his words. Suddenly, it's like I no longer have the capacity for the same type of fury that erupted out of me at the wake. Even the thought that he may end up stuck here too, unable to move on, doesn't elicit the fear I feel it should. I just feel numb. It's over, and not in a way that is satisfying or brings much closure to anyone.

"Hey, it may not be too late," Art tries to encourage me. He takes ahold of my hand again and gently tugs my arm so I'm facing him. His other hand caresses my cheek again. I lean into the heat and softness of his palm. The knot that formed in my stomach begins to unwind. He continues, "The man couldn't even light a box on fire. You think he's going to be able to put a bullet into his own head or tie his own noose?"

A smile at his dark humor stubbornly breaks through my passivity. And although he did have a lightness to his voice as if he were joking, I feel how sure he is and begin to adopt that certainty myself.

"Right, they could still find him before he builds up enough courage to do it," I say, coming out of my slump as if awakening from an unplanned nap.

"So let's follow them. Wouldn't want you to miss them hauling his ass out of the woods and throwing him in the back of that cruiser," Art replies as a satisfied grin spreads across his face. He brings his hand that was cradling my face down to grab ahold of my other hand. Squeezing both of my hands, he looks to me to guide us to the place of my death.

I take a moment to appreciate Art's presence here with me. I give silent thanks to the universe for the connection between us that brought him to me so I didn't have to do any of this on my own. I think of how, for two years, he had to navigate a lot on his own—even longer than that, considering what he said about his mom seemingly abandoning him in the hospital—and I again demand the universe to not leave him behind this time. I only want to pass over into whatever life comes after this with Art by my side.

I maneuver our hands so they hang by our sides with our fingers laced together and take another small step towards him. I look up into his tranquil eyes and take a deep breath to center myself.

"You're right. I wouldn't want to miss that," I agree.

I squeeze his hands as I close my eyes and bring my mind back to the night I died. The flashes of awareness I had as Dale drove me into the mountains and carried me to the clearing in the woods where the river bends replay behind my eyes. I freeze the picture of the clearing in my mind.

Just as I envision the two of us appearing there, Art pulls me into an embrace. I cling to him gratefully for a few moments before I open my eyes to the scenic location of my death.

There's significantly more snow than there was the last time I was here. Then it had been a thin layer, similar to what the town was now getting. At least double the amount of snow now blankets the ground, and it's been recently disturbed. Footprints are trampled into the snow, many on top of each other, like someone has been pacing.

I hear him still pacing a few yards away, the snow swishing around his feet. I hesitantly lift my head in his direction, and my eyes go wide. I can't say I'm surprised at his appearance, considering that the last couple of times I've seen him he's looked like a total wreck—and he wasn't exactly well put together to begin with—but it's becoming clear he was able to hide the extent of his breakdown the last time Winslow and Dennis surprised him at his house. The person in front of me now seems like a man on the brink of insanity. He's glancing around frantically with wide, bloodshot eyes, head whipping around at any small noise. I'm fairly certain he hasn't changed his clothes since seeing me in his cabin and chasing me into the woods, and he definitely hasn't shaved. His wiry beard is kinked in some areas and patchy in others, which I assume is from him pulling his own hairs out as he is currently twisting strands around his finger. He's also deathly pale and visibly trembling. How much of that is from the cold, I'm not sure, but I have a feeling it's only a small percentage. In one of his unsteady hands, he grips a gun, which glints in the light of the setting sun.

Although he came up here with a gun, presumably to blow his brains out, he doesn't notice me or Art in his frantic scanning of the woods around him. Meaning either our theory about people ready to give up on life being able to see us is incorrect ... or he doesn't want to die.

Sounds of fast approaching footsteps bring Dale into a renewed state of panic. His pacing quickens as he begins muttering under his breath. I look on disgusted as I notice a steady string of drool leaking from between his lips. Because of that distraction, it takes me a minute to realize his mutterings are directed to me. He still doesn't see me, but he's speaking to me as if in prayer.

"Hannah, I'm so sorry. Hannah, please forgive me. Hannah, I didn't mean to. Hannah, I'm not a bad man. Hannah, let me go. Hannah, please leave me alone," he chants over and over under his breath.

Seeing me in the woods outside his cabin seems to have broken him. I feel a maniacal smile spreading on my face and try my best to reel it in, but the fact he's being haunted by me with no effort on my part makes bubbles of laughter float up my throat.

The urge to laugh disappears when Winslow and Dennis burst into the clearing. Dale immediately puts the gun to his head. The muzzle pressed hard against his temple for accuracy since his hand is shaking. Winslow and Dennis quickly freeze, and all is very still and quiet for a few moments before Winslow begins trying to deescalate the situation.

"Mr. Evans, please put the gun down and come with us. We'll bring you somewhere warm, get you a nice hot coffee, and you can tell us all about what's going on. Okay?"

Dale shakes his head wildly, his skin puckering around the muzzle as he pushes it even harder against his temple, and replies, "Don't want to talk about it. Can't. It wasn't supposed to happen. I never wanted to kill her, never."

Winslow nods and sympathy radiates from him. I can't tell if he's wielding it like a weapon to weaken Dale's defenses or if he is simply that empathetic. He seems like a seasoned detective, which means he's been subjected countless times to the horrors born from the complexities of human emotion. I watched and read a lot of true crime content in the past, and it seems to me the most atrocious crimes are often committed due to emotions like anger and even love, emotions we all experience countless times in our lives. Criminals are not emotionless monsters. They actually let emotions take over and lose all self-control. Looking at Dale, I don't see the boogeyman. I see a deeply cracked human being. Dangerous, but still just a man.

"Look at me, Dale. Listen to me," Winslow says firmly, but any edge in his voice is softened by his gentle gaze. "I know you didn't want to kill her, Dale. So, why don't you tell me what went wrong?"

Ignoring the question, Dale stutters out, "Sh-she came b-back for me. Ha-Hannah wants m-me dead." He clenches his eyes shut and steadies his hand. "It's only fair."

A shot tears apart the silence of the woods, traveling amongst the trees like a messenger reporting the event to those too far away to witness it firsthand.

17

A scream claws at my throat, but I choke it back down as I hear Dale screaming in pain and see a blossom of red soaking his jacket just below his elbow.

I had been so focused on him I didn't notice Dennis draw his weapon. Now he trudges over and picks up the gun that Dale dropped. He passes it to Winslow, then takes his cuffs from his waistbelt. He clicks one cuff around the wrist of Dale's good arm and one around his own wrist.

"Walk," Dennis demands. He moves the arm connected to Dale by the cuffs sharply forward, yanking him into a standing position from where he was leaning against a tree and cradling his damaged arm.

They make their way back to the road in silence. Dale lags behind Dennis as much as the cuffs allow, hoping for a brief pause in their trek, but Dennis pulls him along and gives no response to Dale's increasing complaints about feeling weak.

Winslow promises Dale he will tend to his arm once they reach the cruiser, and he does. Once they reach the car, Winslow retrieves a first-aid kit from the trunk as Dennis puts Dale in the backseat and untethers himself from him, transferring the cuff on his wrist to the partition between the front half of the car and the backseat. He leaves the door open for Winslow to provide first aid to Dale's arm.

Winslow examines the wound, and notes that the bullet went straight through and was already beginning to clot. He wraps it tight with gauze, secures it, and promises they'll get an actual doctor to tend to it back in town.

Winslow draws back to close the door, but Dale grabs his wrist and looks up at him with wet eyes.

"I wasn't going to kill her, but she took off my mask. She saw my face. She could identify me, but even worse, she never would have looked at me the same way again," Dale says.

Winslow holds eye contact with Dale for a few moments then nods. Dale lets go of Winslow's wrist when he realizes that's the only response he'll be getting, and both detectives get into the car and drive off, finally able to bring answers to a town that has been anxiously awaiting the conclusion of this case.

I watch as the car disappears down the mountain, then join Art where he leans against the hood of Dale's truck. Seeing the rickety, old thing again, the wheezing sounds I heard it make through my haze of semi-consciousness as it struggled up the road emerges from that suppressed memory. That noise, which seemed to promise imminent mechanical failure, fills my brain for a short moment before fading into the back of my mind again.

I approach Art, whose head is angled down, hair obscuring his eyes. I can see he's biting his lip and picking at his nails on one hand. One of his legs bounces with a quick, jittery rhythm. His eyes dart around and behind me but never fully land on me as I come near. Once I'm right in front of him, he looks back down at his feet again. I slip my hand into the hand he's nervously picking at and ask him what's wrong.

"Have you seen anything yet?" he asks. He doesn't need to elaborate.

I cup his chin in my other hand and lift his head so he's looking at me, then I move my hand up to cup his cheek and brush my thumb along its soft surface.

"I haven't seen it," I say.

"You're sure?" he asks.

"Yes, Art, I'm positive. I think there's still a bit more for me here. Dale isn't officially behind bars yet. Plus, I'm pretty sure the universe and I have come to an understanding. I'm not following any light that you can't see. I'm not leaving you, Arthur," I reply.

"The more you say that, the more I believe it could actually be possible," Art says as he gazes into my eyes.

"How many more times do you think I need to say it before you believe it fully?" I ask.

"I don't know," Art replies with a sad smile, but his eyes sparkle when he places his palm against my cheek and feels me lean into his touch.

"I'll say it as many times as I need to. I won't leave you, Arthur," I say.

"You know, for as long as I can remember I preferred my nickname. I really like when you call me Arthur though," he says and rests his forehead against mine.

Unable to think of anything to say in response, I move my arms to wrap around his neck. He moves his to encircle my waist, and I nestle into his familiar warmth. Butterflies flutter around in my stomach and my brain, erasing all thoughts so I can focus solely on the feeling of Art's arms around me and his breath against my lips every time he exhales.

We stay like this for several moments, appreciating each other's presence and steadily growing warmth. Then, Art pulls me in even closer and leans his face forward to the point where our noses are now touching as well. I hold my breath, waiting for his lips to connect with mine. But they don't.

Instead he pulls back and says, "There's somewhere I want to take you. Is that okay? Or do you want to follow the detectives and see what happens with Dale?"

I take a deep breath to dispel the slight dizziness from my unresolved anticipation.

"No, I'm sure we have plenty of time before anything major happens," I say.

"Cool," Art says with a grin. I lose the weight of his arms around me as he lets go of my waist to hold my hands. He looks at our connected hands for a moment before focusing back on me.

His excitement is evident in every aspect of his demeanor. I can see it in the sparkle of his eyes; can feel it in the way he's squeezing my hands. It all pours into the wide smile that appears on his face as he looks at me.

"Close your eyes," he says.

I comply and try to tune out all background noise to focus on the sound of his steady breathing. Therefore it takes me a second to realize I can hear waves crashing instead of leaves rustling in the breeze.

"You can open now," Art tells me.

The scene that I open my eyes to makes my breath catch in my throat. We are standing on golden sand with a vast expanse of vividly blue water sparkling in the sun and stretching out to the horizon in front of us. On one end of the beach, there's a castle-like tower sitting atop an outcropping of rock. A mountain borders the other end, imposing and majestic.

I look over to Art with my mouth agape.

"This is the most beautiful place I've ever seen," I say.

Art smiles proudly and says, "I was hoping you'd think so. I couldn't agree more."

I take another look around, marveling at the beauty of it all. Then I take a moment to gaze at Art. His eyes are closed and face pointed towards the sea. The breeze whips his hair back, giving me a clear look at his beautiful profile. His high cheekbones, sharp jawline, and perfectly curved nose are like you would see on a Greek statue. Every feature flawless, like he was sculpted by the Gods themselves. Something in his stance makes me think of an otherworldly royalty, as if he were a son of Poseidon gifted this beautiful coast to rule over. He would be such a gracious ruler. People would be tripping over themselves to leave him offerings, and praises would rain from their tongues constantly.

I have an overwhelming urge to nestle my head in the swan-like swoop of his neck and trail kisses up its length, and I nearly take a step towards him. Before I do, his eyes open and focus on me.

Even with embarrassment at being caught staring at him flooding through my system, my body won't listen to my brain begging to turn away in shame. Instead, my body goes rigid, cementing me in place, and my gaze does not falter.

He grins at me, and I catch a glimpse of mischief flash in his eyes for the briefest moment. Enough to make me want to melt into a puddle to be absorbed by the sand. If there was still blood in my veins, I'm positive it would have rushed to my cheeks. I give silent thanks that I'm at least not that transparent. My body is speaking for itself enough as it is anyway.

I force myself to look away and ask, "Where are we?"

"We're in Italy," Art says.

I look back to him in amazement, and his smile spreads.

"I've never been out of the country before," I say.

"We only came once. I was about eight years old, I think. It was a family trip to meet my dad's parents. He brought us to this beach and said he used to play here all the time when he was little. We came here every day during that trip."

He sits in the sand, his legs splayed out in front of him, elbows resting on his knees. I sit beside him with my legs straight out in front of me and lean back onto my elbows.

"I can see why. It's so stunning," I say.

He nods and continues, "I was a bit scared of the water. I think I was used to the lake, and being able to see to the other side. When you look out over the ocean, there doesn't seem to be an end to it. So, I was always nervous to get in. My mom would carry me in on her back. She'd say, 'Hold onto me tight and I'll hold onto you tight. That way, no wave can tear us apart.'"

At the mention of his mother, I sit up straight and turn my full attention to him. He's gazing out over the water with an impassive expression, but his hands are shaking. He tries to hide it by clutching them together between his knees.

"She would walk us in and wait for me to relax. We'd sway along with the water as we watched my dad and brothers get rowdier, usually turning into a splash war. Once I loosened up enough to throw a few splashes into the mix, she'd get more playful. Jostle me around on her back and twirl me. She'd hold me by my arms and spin, and I'd unwrap my legs from around her waist to trail out behind me. I'd latch back on after, but at that point I wasn't scared. I just wanted to be close to her. And she never let go or complained a single time."

I reach my arm across the space between us and place my hand on his knee. He lays one of his hands on top of mine. It isn't shaking anymore.

"Sounds like a lot of good memories here," I say.

"Yeah," he says. His fingers glide over mine, back and forth, just barely making contact with my skin. Still, my hand feels electrified.

"I haven't let myself think of the good memories, at least not of her, for a long while. But something about being with you draws them out of me," he says.

I smile and turn my hand over. He traces lazy circles against my palm before curling his fingers between mine.

"After seeing how that note on Dale's door drained everything out of you, then being in the middle of that standoff, I just wanted to give you some peace. Remind you it's not all bad" he says.

"And this place came to mind," I say.

"Most peaceful place I've ever been."

"I can easily agree with that."

"There was this one time where I was walking along the shoreline. I didn't mind so much being close to the water, but I was constantly looking back at my mom laid out on her towel, and she was always watching me too. Anyway, this one time, I cut the bottom of my foot on a broken seashell. I fell down in tears immediately. I went to turn around to cry out for her, and she was already there, bending over to pick me up. I had to get a couple stitches. As it was healing, it was painful to walk on and annoying to limp around on my heel. I would get so frustrated," he says, but it turns into a chuckle at the end.

"Not all bad, huh? Even paradise made you bleed," I say, but when he turns to look at me, there's a smile on my face as well.

"That's life though," he says. His smile stays on his face, though it softens and his eyes lose a bit of their humorous sparkle. "There's always a little bit of pain, even amidst all the beauty. It doesn't lessen the pleasure. I think I can finally see that they can live side by side. You showed me that. So, I wanted to show you this."

I lay my head on his shoulder and whisper, "Thank you." He says nothing but rests his head against mine. I close my eyes and feel the ebb and flow of our gratefulness for each other moving between us, smoothing away the jagged edges of hopelessness, despair, and loneliness that had been threatening to permanently scar our hearts. I don't allow any thoughts of Dale or doubts about whether or not I ever deserved Bobbi's kindness to infiltrate my thoughts, and I hope Art isn't allowing himself to dwell on any negative memories of his mother or worry about me moving on without him. This is the first moment since I woke up after death that I have been able to clear my mind and immerse myself in the moment with no concern for what is to come next. I hold tight to Art's hand and breathe.

I open my eyes to the waves once more, watching them rise and fall long enough to match my inhales and exhales with their rhythm, until I remember the tower. It's an intriguing feature of the beach I didn't take enough time to appreciate during the initial shock of our arrival. I lean back to look over Art's shoulders and feel him shiver as my hair brushes along his neck. I'm glad he can't see my face, because I can't stop myself from grinning.

"What do you think that tower is for?" I ask.

"Could be a watchtower, or maybe used to be one. I don't know if it's still in use. It's not open for the public," he says.

"I don't think that applies to us though," I say.

He turns around to look at me, and I wink up at him before getting to my feet.

"You coming?" I ask and extend my arm down to him.

He chuckles as he takes my hand and says, "Yeah, sure. Why not?"

We walk to the tower hand in hand, pausing occasionally to look at seashells, a washed-up jellyfish, and a crab scurrying back into the water.

The small walk to the tower is more eventful than our exploration of the building. It's mostly bare inside other than a few tables with outdated machinery on top, some chairs, and dusty shelves emptied of the daily logs I assume were kept there.

The light filtering in from the windows dims with the setting sun, casting the place in shadows. We stay peering out the observation windows facing the sea until the shadows overtake the room.

I'm about to suggest going back home when a faint light dispels the darkness of the doorway which leads to other barren rooms we peeked at earlier. The light seems to be walking up the short hallway towards this room. I glance at Art and see he's also focused on the door.

I turn my attention back to the door just as a man, dressed in centuries-old clothing and carrying a lantern, rounds the corner and enters the room. It isn't only his wardrobe that makes it clear he isn't a modern caretaker. He's also blinking in and out of existence as he walks across the room to the windows overlooking the ocean.

I try to get his attention as he passes us, but he has no reaction.

At the window, he takes a small pair of binoculars out of his coat pocket and examines the horizon for several moments. Then he sits at a nearby desk and appears to write in a book that isn't visible to me. After making his notes, he takes up his lantern again and disappears back down the hallway.

Art and I stand amongst the relics of another time in silence. The room, once again empty, feels less abandoned now, but I don't know if that makes it more or less ominous. Perhaps it's just the darkness that's unnerving me. Nothing the apparition did was unsettling, except the way he stuttered in and out of focus. Regardless, he's gone now, and the shadows are becoming so thick I feel like I could suffocate.

I flail my arm out in Art's direction. When I feel his familiar, comforting grip on my hand, I lead us out the small building and head back toward the shore. Out of the shadows, enveloped by the light of the moon, I relax. I slow my pace and look at Art. The way the moon spotlights his face combined with his pensive expression brings to mind the statue of The Thinker.

"What are you thinking?" I ask.

After a moment of silence, he answers with his own question, "Why do you think he couldn't see us?"

An explanation for this question had already come to mind as I watched the figure go about his work after he failed to respond to me.

"I don't think he was like us," I say. "He was more like an imprint. I've read before that sometimes people leave behind a trace of themselves after they've moved on, like a memory that's played on repeat. The book that I read claimed they fade in time. It has to fade in order for the soul to fully ascend to the next plane of existence."

"Do you think we'll leave behind a trace?" he asks.

I think for a moment before saying, "I suppose it could happen."

"And when it fades completely, we're gone for good from this life? Will we remember any of it? Do you think we'll take who we were here with us to wherever it is we end up after passing over?" he asks.

We walk in silence down the length of shoreline as I mull over these questions. He doesn't rush me.

"I don't know what comes next. Maybe we'll forget, maybe we

won't. Maybe reincarnation is real and we'll start a new life. But I do know we won't be erased. The people who love us will remember us and talk about us and think of us. The us that are present right now will live on that way, and I think that's enough," I say.

He nods and takes a moment to gather his thoughts before saying, "I know none of us can say for sure what's waiting for us, but is there a theory you lean towards or hope is true?"

"I think I lean towards reincarnation," I say.

"What would you want to come back as?" he asks.

"I think I'd like to take another shot at being a human. So I can work towards being nicer to the people in my life ... and to myself," I say.

"I like the sound of that, especially the last bit," Art says and squeezes my hand.

I stop walking. My arm extends between us like a tether as he takes another step before realizing I stopped. He turns back and searches my face. I don't know what he's looking for, but he takes a small step forward to see me more clearly in the moonlight.

"There's something I've been wanting to ask you," I say. My nerves make my voice shake.

He closes the remaining distance between us to cup my face in his palm and look into my eyes.

"What is it?" he asks. His voice sounds huskier than I've heard it before, sending a shiver up my spine.

"Have you wondered why you were drawn to where I was? Why you felt that pull only to show up in a place you've never been to help a girl you've never met?" I ask.

"At first," he says. "I got there before you ... woke up? I'm not really sure what to call it. When you sat up out of your body at the morgue. Before that, before actually meeting you, I wondered why I was drawn there."

"And now? Do you think it was because you could help me? Or do you think it could be ... something more? Maybe because we ..." I trail off, hoping he will share the same feeling I've felt ever since I first looked into his mesmerizing eyes and felt at peace.

With his gaze melting into mine, the worry that he doesn't feel the same as I do drains away. The magic of his eyes working on me yet again. I savor every moment until my meditation is broken by his reply.

"Because we're connected," he says.

"You feel it too?" I ask, relief lifting my voice.

"Almost since the moment I saw you," he replies. "It was like I recognized you. But not you, exactly. Something deeper. Something … molecular. And the longer we spend together, the stronger that feeling gets. I feel like I've known you for ages. And I would do anything for you. Anything to keep you near me. Because I finally feel like I've found where I belong. With you."

I let go of his hand so I can hold his face in both of mine. I trace small circles on his cheek with my thumb before bringing my hands together behind his neck and nuzzling my face against his chest.

He holds me for a few moments then takes my chin in his fingers and tilts my head up. His face is right above mine, closer than ever before. I feel his lips ghost over mine but, before they can connect fully, our attention is pulled toward the sky where the sun passes quickly across the sky twice before coming to rest low in the east. It's morning, and it's been two days since Dale was driven into town in the back of the detectives' car.

Art and I look at each other again. My eyes are drawn to his lips that I so nearly got to taste. I take in the way they move as he speaks before I register the words themselves.

"We should probably go. Something is bound to be happening by now," he says.

"Right," I say. "Time to go."

We leave the beach behind and find ourselves in a court-room.

Dale sits behind the defendant's table next to his lawyer, who is scanning over his notes and shuffling through the case file. My mother is beside the prosecutor at the other table. They're speaking to each other in low tones with their heads bent together.

When the judge enters the room, everyone stops shuffling and whispering to focus their attention on him as he ascends to his bench.

"Good morning, everyone. Let's begin, shall we?" the judge says once he's seated. He states the case then says, "I've been informed an agreement has been made?" At this, he looks up from his papers and out at the defense attorney and the prosecutor expectantly.

"Yes, Your Honor," Dale's lawyer says. "My client would like to plead guilty to the charges of aggravated assault, kidnapping, rape, and felony murder."

The judge turns his gaze on Dale and begins a string of questions to make certain that he is aware of the rights he is giving up by pleading guilty. Dale responds with a quiet but sure "yes" to each question asked, then he is brought forward to testify under oath to the facts regarding his guilt.

"On the night of November thirteenth, I entered the home of Hannah King and Julien Stoll with the purpose of kidnapping and raping Hannah. After assaulting Mr. Stoll, I took Hannah into the woods up the mountain, which is where I raped her. Then I- she took off the mask I was wearing, so I ... I killed her."

My mother shudders but holds back her tears.

The judge watches Dale with a face like stone. Nothing in his expression conveys his thoughts, which I find myself wondering if judges have special training on how to keep an unbiased image.

When Dale finishes his statement, the judge nods once then looks to the prosecutor.

"The defendant has entered his plea, is there anything else to add?" he asks.

"Only one thing, Your Honor," the prosecutor says. "Although we know the decision is ultimately yours to make, Ms. King would like to have it on record that she does not wish to seek the death penalty as the sentence for this case."

Dale's head snaps in my mother's direction, and his eyes begin to waver behind tears.

"Does that mean you've forgiven me, Carolyn?" he asks. However, his hopeful smile is obliterated by the boiling gaze my mom turns on him.

"How dare you ask me that," she says. "I don't want you to get the death penalty because I don't think you deserve an easy death."

Dale flinches at her scalding tone and curls in on himself like a cowering child.

"I want you to rot in a jail cell. I want you to suffer through every sleepless night where Hannah haunts your dreams," she continues.

"Ms. King, that's enough," the judge warns.

The prosecutor puts a hand on her shoulder which she shoves off as she gets to her feet.

Her voice raises as she continues, "You obsessed over her for God knows how long, so I want you to keep thinking about her. I want you afraid to even blink for fear of seeing her behind your eyelids. I want you to die with her plaguing your every thought."

"Order!" the judge's shout rings throughout the room.

My mom takes a deep breath and allows herself to be guided back into her chair.

"I'm sorry, Your Honor," she says to the judge.

"I know the circumstances are extremely distressing, so I'm letting you off with a warning. No more outbursts. And you," he turns his attention to Dale. "No more instigating. Keep your mouth shut unless you're spoken to. Understood?"

"Yes, Your Honor. I'm sorry," Dale says.

The judge stays quiet for a few moments, perhaps wanting them to both stew in their feelings after being chastised. Then he says, "If everyone has said their piece, we will adjourn and schedule a sentencing hearing in two weeks."

When no one objects, he continues, "During that time, I want a presentence report prepared. From the prosecution, I want a detailed breakdown of all the evidence in this case and how they relate to Mr. Evans. Understood?"

The defense attorney and prosecutor give their assent, and the judge declares the court adjourned.

Two prison guards come in to collect Dale. They clamp cuffs onto his hands and feet then shuffle him out of the court room. He keeps his head pointed down, eyes glued to his feet, as he passes my mom. Her eyes drill into his back until he is escorted out the side door. I glimpse a prison van idling before the door closes with a *thunk*. The dull note echoing throughout the empty room has a sense of finality.

Before the judge disappears into a back office, he calls out to my mom, "Stay out of trouble, Ms. King." His words are half joke, half warning.

She looks into his eyes and nods. A silent second ticks by, then she opens her mouth to give a more respectful answer. Except the judge must have been satisfied with the nod, as he is already through the doorway and pulling the door shut behind him.

"May I walk you to your car, Ms. King?" the prosecutor asks.

"As long as you don't chastise me as well," she replies. The lawyer presses his lips together in an attempt to keep the reprimand in. My mom notices and sighs. "It won't happen again, I promise. What he said ... it was just very unexpected and infuriating."

The lawyer's face softens, and he says, "I understand, and I doubt Mr. Evans will make a similar outburst again. Still, remember to keep your composure. The judge won't be so lenient the next time."

"Yes, I know and I will," my mom says.

"Still willing to let me be your escort?" the lawyer asks.

My mom looks at his earnest face and relaxes. She chuckles and agrees, taking the arm he extends to her.

Art and I follow my mom home, and I'm happy to see my aunt is back. She rushes to my mom's side as soon as she walks through the door.

"So, how did it go?" my aunt asks.

My mom recounts how Dale pleaded guilty to all charges and how the judge scheduled the sentencing to take place in two weeks, but leaves out the fact that she verbally assaulted Dale in front of the judge.

My aunt seems disappointed that the judge didn't sentence Dale today. Most likely she won't be able to stay for two weeks.

"Did you mention that you didn't want to pursue the death penalty?" she asks.

"Yeah, the lawyer did. It is still ultimately up to the judge though," my mom says.

"Well, you know how I feel about it," my aunt says.

"Yes, I do. And you know that I respectfully disagree."

"What if he gets parole, Carolyn?"

"He's got four charges against him, Claire. You still have to serve a minimum number of years for each crime before being considered for parole, and these are felony crimes. He'll be locked away for life. I just know it. And hey, his dad died fairly young from prostate cancer. You never know."

"It's probably a bad idea to pray for someone to contract a deadly disease, huh?"

"Mmm, let's just keep our fingers crossed, yeah?"

My aunt consents, giving my mom a reassuring smile and pulling her into a hug. She pulls back to ask my mom if she wants some coffee.

"I put some on to brew around the time I thought you'd be finished up at court," she says.

"That would be lovely," my mom says and sinks into a chair at the kitchen table.

"What about that lawyer?" my aunt asks as she mixes my mom's cup the way she likes it.

"What about him?" my mom asks.

"Is he cute?"

"Oh, don't start."

"Come on! Indulge me."

"He's too young for me."

"What about Winslow?" my aunt asks as she carries both cups of coffee to the table and sits next to my mom.

"John is a professional. He'd never ask out a client," my mom says.

"Would you want him to, though?" my aunt asks.

My mom shakes her head, whether in denial or exasperation I can't tell, then says, "Imagine trying to explain to people how we met. 'Oh, well he was the lead detective on my daughter's murder case.' I would get depressed any time someone asked or any time I thought about how he came into my life."

"You're right. I'm sorry," my aunt says. She places her hand over my mom's and squeezes. "I know you've never needed a man in your life before anyway. It's just ... I hate to think of you here all alone. Will you come to Colorado after the sentencing? Come stay with me? See the kids?"

"Yes, I'd love that," my mom answers. She turns her hand over underneath my aunt's so they can clasp onto each other.

"You're welcome to stay as long as you want," my aunt says.

I smile at the sight of them. Their hands stay clasped together as they continue to drink their coffee in silence. Hearing my mom say she'd go stay with Aunt Claire lifted a weight from my soul. I haven't realized just how worried I've been about my mom being on her own until now. I have a renewed sense of gratefulness for my aunt, and I'm proud of my mom for allowing herself to be cared for.

I leave them to their coffee and each other's company and lead Art to my room again. I flop onto my back on the bed while Art perches on the edge.

"Art, you can lay back if you want," I say.

He lowers himself, but he seems stiff.

I slip my hand into his and feel him relax.

He turns his head to look at me and says, "Sorry if I seem a bit hot and cold towards you sometimes. It's like ... I feel strongly drawn to you but, the closer I get to you, the more I'm reminded that we don't have much time. Then I feel like I need to pull back because it's going to hurt enough as it is to lose you."

I roll on my side to face him and say, "It's okay, Arthur. I understand. It's a confusing situation. But just know—" I pause to place my other hand on his cheek. I stroke my thumb along his cheekbone and continue, "Even if we are separated after we pass over, we'll find each other again. Even if we aren't aware of it, we'll be searching for each other. And when we find each other again, we'll know. Our souls will know."

Art turns on his side as well and reaches his arm across the space between us to wrap his arm around my waist. He pulls me closer to him, and I tuck my head under his chin, burying my face into his chest.

"What are we going to do for two weeks?" I ask. After thinking for a moment, I add, "Assuming time doesn't speed up again."

"It never does when you want it to," Art says.

I bunch his shirt in my fists behind his back and press myself further into him.

"I don't know if I want it to," I say.

Art runs his fingers through my hair with his free hand. The arm wrapped around my shoulders closes more securely around me. His hold on me feels protective, and I can't help but sigh with how content I feel in his arms.

"Well, to answer your question, we can still keep track of what's going on," Art says. "The prosecutor will probably be working with Winslow and Dennis. Whoever is in charge of the presentence report will be interviewing Dale pretty consistently I think but also anyone who was acquainted with him to fill in his background."

"Always thinking, aren't you?" I say and look up at him with a smile on my face. He smiles back, and I continue, "I don't want to think today though. Let's just be lazy. We can get back to eavesdropping tomorrow."

And so we do.

Each day we check in with Winslow and Dennis, the prosecutor, the progress of the presentence report and, of course, my mom. We also allow ourselves "lazy time" throughout the days. Whether that's lounging around my room or taking strolls around the town and talking.

Art shares more happy stories involving his mother during our walks. Like a memory he has of a Christmas when he was a child where she somehow got him the remote control R2-D2 he desperately wanted even though they were tight on money that year. Or the time she slept outside with him in a small tent during one of their trips to the lake house. Or how she went all out for his high school graduation, waking him up with confetti poppers and a massive breakfast. Or, another Christmas, where she went overboard with all the dishes and desserts she made. She pushed more and more food on them until they were nauseous, and there was still enough left over to last the entire following week.

The stories often leave me with aching cheeks from laughing. There is a steady smile on my face when we get these moments, because I'm so glad that Art is embracing these memories instead of ignoring them or turning them sour by dwelling on what happened between them at the end.

We never learn anything new from seeing Winslow and Dennis as they work with the prosecutor. Their meetings have a lot to do with organizing all the evidence, linking them all together clearly, and answering any questions the lawyer asks as he works on his speech for the court. His goal is to show that a majority of Dale's crimes were carefully planned out and executed ruthlessly and so he should be given the maximum punishment for every crime with no possibility for parole.

Listening in on the interviews with Dale for the presentence report is usually the most interesting part of the day. Especially when they talk about his mental state before, during, and after the crimes. Dale consistently declares that he was fully aware throughout the whole process that his actions were wrong and would result in serious legal consequences if he were caught. When asked about his suicide attempt and why he told Winslow I had come back for him, he told them the stress of thinking "will they come for me today?" stripped him mentally. The fear of being found out and the guilt he struggled with daily made him act irrationally. Whether he believes that chasing me through his house and seeing me in the woods was only a delusion or he *wants* to believe it, I can't say. The toppled lamp and crooked front door seem hard to dismiss. Perhaps he isn't telling them about that incident because he doesn't want to be written off as mentally unstable. Does he want a full, fair sentence because he feels guilty? Or is he looking for notoriety?

The other people they interview for the presentence report all have loose links to Dale, so they don't have much to say about him, good or bad. Most of them describe him as a loner. A quiet type who kept to himself and only spoke when spoken to. No one ever saw him get into a fight, not even when drunk. No one ever saw him get angry or even agitated. He was just the sort of man that was there in the background. Nobody can fathom how this tragic act of violence came from this man, but no one pities him. There is disgust and rage on each face as they speak of him. Not a single one of them claim he's a good man. They all want to see him get his due.

Every day, after making our rounds, Art and I go back to my mom's house. Aunt Claire leaves at the end of the first week to go back to Colorado. Bobbi and her mom visit often throughout the two weeks.

Although I'm still nervous about what is going to happen once all of this is over, I do want it to be finished for my mom's sake. I get antsy for the sentencing to happen as the days tick by so that she can take her trip to Colorado. She needs that time away.

With two days to go before the sentencing, Art can see how restless I am and suggests we get away until the hearing.

We go back to the beach for the first day and explore the entire shoreline. Curious, I make my way into the water until it's up to my hips. I let the waves roll through me and feel a deep sense of connection with the universe and everything in it. It's as if a secret knowledge is being shared with me as the slow, majestic motion of the waves flow in and out of me. I think of the fish that follow these currents like a road, trusting it to guide them rather than navigate blind. Which leads me to think of birds using wind currents in the same way, and how the wind influences the sea. I sense millions of similar connections shaping the world and, for once in my life, feel like I am a part of it.

Art wades in beside me and takes my hand as we sway with the waves.

He whispers, "This feels ..."

After a moment of waiting for him to continue, I say, "Like the universe is moving through you."

"Exactly like that," Art says.

I can feel his gaze on me and am drawn to it like a sunflower to the sun. When our eyes meet, I angle myself towards him and reach out. My hands travel up his arms to rest just below his elbows.

He pulls me closer and lowers his head until his forehead rests against mine. We stay in this embrace for several moments, taking the time to focus on one another as well as the feel of the water moving through us both.

After trudging back to shore, we notice no water has seeped into our clothes or clung to our skin. We are as dry as the sand beneath our feet, which also does not stick to us.

"I like the beach a lot better this way. I always hated how sand would get into every little crevice," I say.

Art laughs and agrees as he leads me to a cozy spot where the beach slopes up toward the mountain giving us an expansive view of the horizon as the sun lowers to kiss the waves and make them golden.

We spend the night stargazing, but I often turn my attention to the tower on the other side of the beach, searching for a flicker of light from within. It stays dark all night however, and I wonder if it's because we're too far away or if the man, whoever he was, has finally abandoned his post.

19

Our second day away we go back to the lake house. This time he takes me on a short tour of the inside. It's clear it's been a while since anyone from his family has made use of it, but it's also far from abandoned. There are signs of life, like toys strewn about in one of the rooms, precisely-made beds, and a DVD collection displayed in the living room organized alphabetically for easy selection. There is, however, a thin but noticeable accumulation of dust on many surfaces and a slight musty scent to the air.

We spend the rest of our time outside, walking the perimeter of the lake and seeking out any little critter we hear shuffling around. Art surprises me with his expansive knowledge of birds. He identifies every one we see, no matter how brief a glance we get. It turns out that bird watching was another thing he and his mother used to do together.

"Especially here, there are so many different kinds of birds in these mountains," Art says. He looks fondly around and up at the canopy of leaves above us then continues, "We made time for it nearly every day of our vacation. My brothers used to tease me about it, but it really did fascinate me. Still does. Plus, it was nice to get away from them for a while. They could be a bit overwhelming. Mostly though, it was nice to have alone time with my mom. I'm the youngest in the family, so her attention was usually split three ways. I liked when it was fully on me."

After a moment of silence, I ask, "Do you have a favorite bird?

I don't know much about birds, but my favorite is the blue-footed booby."

Art glances down at me with a teasing grin and asks, "Is it your favorite because it has booby in its name?"

I gasp as if insulted and reply, "Do I really come across as that immature?"

Art's grin spreads, and his eyes twinkle with amusement as I swat at his arm in feigned indignity. He grabs my arm and slides his hand in mine. His arm lifts up over my head and settles behind my back with my arm wrapped around my front, our hands still connected, resting against my other arm.

"You absolutely do not," Art answers. "What is the reason though, since you don't know much about birds? Why that one?"

"I just think they look really goofy and cute," I say.

"That's all it takes, huh?" Art teases.

"Yeah, why else do you think I warmed up to you so fast?" I tease back.

"Oh, so that's how you're gonna be?" Art asks.

I hear a note of mischief in his voice, but before I can pull away, he holds my hand tighter so I can't wiggle away as he tickles me with his free hand.

When he stops, I find myself with my back against a tree and his chest pressed against mine. Our laughter slowly subsides as we gaze into each other's eyes.

To distract myself from the overwhelming urge to kiss him, I ask, "So, what's your favorite then?"

The look he gives me makes my stomach feel so airy that I think I may float away. Because he looks at me like nothing before this moment holds any space in his head. Like the only thing he can remember is the color of my eyes.

I try to sound nonchalant when I answer his questioning gaze by adding, "Birds, remember? What's your favorite?"

"Ah, yes, of course. I've always loved ravens. They're super smart, and they have quite the reputation in literature. Either a harbinger of death or the right-hand man, or woman, to numerous Gods around the world," Art says.

I smile at his enthusiasm as we begin walking again, talking about birds the whole way back to the cabin. There, we settle on the porch in silence.

After sitting quietly long enough for the gentle rocking of the porch swing to have put me to sleep if I were still capable, Art breaks the silence.

"I remember, when I brought you here before, you wanted me to talk about my mom," he says.

"Yeah, unsuccessfully. But I did get you to sing again," I say.

"That you did," he says with a smile. He starts fidgeting with my fingers as he continues. "You didn't just want to hear stories though, like the ones I've been telling you. You wanted me to think more about how she was when I was in the hospital, to try to understand her. I cut you off before, but I think that's what you were going to ask."

He looks to me for confirmation, and I nod.

"I was going to suggest that perhaps she just couldn't handle losing her husband and her son so close together," I say. I look into his eyes and see the same pain I have seen in the past when his mom has been mentioned, but it isn't as sharp or consuming as it used to be. I hope it's because talking about the good memories has allowed him to at least begin to forgive her. "It's not really an excuse, it doesn't make the pain go away, but it is an explanation. One that makes more sense than her simply deciding to abandon you."

"I don't think I ever believed she bailed for any other reason than it hurt her to be there, but that didn't lessen the anger I felt towards her. Because I was scared and in pain too, more so than her. At least, that's what I told myself. That my physical pain trumped her emotional pain. But that's not really how pain works, is it?" He pauses, and I wait a couple moments to see if it's a rhetorical question, or if he wants me to answer. With his eyes averted back down to my hand, he continues, "I'm not scared or in pain anymore though, so I don't want to be angry either. It still hurts, thinking about how I was left alone in that hospital for the last months of my life, but I have tried to put myself in her shoes. I don't think I would have acted the way she did, but I can understand the emotions that led her to it. What really makes me want to let go of the anger is the thought that she may still be feeling those emotions."

Unsure of what to say, I press myself against his side and wrap my arms around him. He hugs me back as we sway in silence once again.

"Have you ever thought about checking on her?" I ask.

"Plenty of times," Art sighs. "Usually, the anger would come rushing back, so I wouldn't go. Now though ... I'm scared of what I might find. Either way, if she's happy or miserable, it's still going to hurt."

"Is there one you would prefer?" I ask.

He pulls away enough to look at my face and says, "I don't want her to be miserable. Of course, I'd rather her be happy. It's just that, a part of me feels like that would mean the reason she left was because she didn't really care."

"Those are intrusive thoughts that feed off of insecurities. They're surface-level thoughts. You've been listening to them for too long," I say and squeeze his hand. Instinctively, I lift his hand to my lips and place a kiss along his knuckles before continuing, "But I do think you're starting to dig deeper. I promise, you'll find that there are reasonable thoughts beneath the shitty ones. For instance, think about all the stories you've been telling me about you and your mom and tell me honestly that you believe she doesn't care for you."

"You're right," he says as he brushes his thumb along my knuckles. "It's just hard for me to let go of the anger and negative thinking because I've been using it as a shield for years now."

"But now you know you don't need that shield, that it's in fact holding you back. It's never easy to shift your way of thinking, but I believe you can. Start with the thought of your mother happy. You said you want her to be happy, and I believe you. From your memories with her, you know she does really care for you. So, where else could that fear be coming from?" I ask.

After taking a moment to think, Art says, "I think I'm actually worried that, if she's no longer grieving, then she'll forget about me."

"And if you dig deeper into that thought, I think you'll find that grief doesn't work like that. A person can be sad with moments of happiness or happy with moments of sadness. If you go to her and find that she seems happy, that doesn't mean she never misses you. Memories of you didn't die when you did. All of those memories you have, she has the same ones and probably thinks of them daily," I say, then I cup his cheek and turn his head to look at me. "A love like that doesn't fade, Arthur."

"You're really good at this," he says as he gazes into my eyes.

"Good at what?" I ask.

"Making me feel better and helping me see the positive side of everything," he answers and begins lightly brushing his fingers through my hair at my temple.

I feel like I could start purring like a cat from how comforting the steady drag of his fingers feel, but instead I say, "I'm glad I can help. I just say what I believe to be the truth."

He pulls me closer again so my head is resting on his chest and says, "You think so highly of me. It makes me want to try harder and be better, so I can actually deserve it."

I bunch his shirt in my fist where it rests on his stomach and say, "You already deserve it, exactly as you are. Arthur, you're one of the best people I've ever met. I don't know how I would've done any of this without you. You've been my rock this entire time."

I look up to see him gazing down at me. His face hovers over me as he bends closer to place a kiss on my forehead. I close my eyes as his lips brush over my skin, and when I open them, he is once again sitting back.

It's dark now, and we both stare out at the lake illuminated by the light of the moon. Mostly full tonight, it hides nothing. The dull, silver light shows us every tree, every bush, and every movement of the nocturnal inhabitants of the lake going about their normal routines.

After another stretch of comfortable silence, Art says, "I do want to check on her."

I straighten up so I can look directly at him and study his face. I don't detect any apprehension in his eyes, and his body isn't rigid with nerves. Just to double check, I ask him if he's sure.

"Yeah, I think I need to. It's long overdue," he says.

I nod and ask, "Do you want me to come with you, or do you need to do this on your own?"

He holds my hand closer to his chest and says, "I want you to come, but I'll understand if you don't want to."

"I'll go anywhere with you, Arthur. This is important to you, so it's important to me too," I say.

He angles his body towards me and takes both my hands in his. I feel him squeeze them briefly, more for his own comfort than mine.

"Ready? Eyes closed," he says, and I shut my eyes along with him.

When I open them a few moments later, I see a small, blue house with a tiny porch. There's an array of windchimes hanging along the front rafter. Below, weeds are running wild in the sad garden of strangled rosebushes.

I look up at Art and notice his jaw is clenched shut, so I give his hand a reassuring squeeze.

"She never let her garden get like this before," he says, worry making his voice shake. "And she moved. This isn't the house I grew up in. Why would she sell and then move into a tiny place like this?"

I have no answer for him, and I know he isn't expecting one from me anyway. The answers are right up those steps, so I ask, "Should we go in?"

He nods and walks up the stairs while also taking in every detail he can, looking for any more signs of neglect. A bird house lays shattered at the far end of the porch, and he stares at it for a few moments before he turns his attention to the front door. It's a plain white door, though it has sun damage so it's not completely white anymore, with nothing decorating it except for a rusty mail slot.

Art takes a deep breath then walks through the door, and I follow directly after him, stepping into the house and onto a pile of mail.

The first thing I notice, other than the envelopes under my feet, is a faint sour smell, like curdled milk mixed with body odor.

My eyes are drawn to the pictures lining the walls to the left beside the door and directly foreword above the couch. They have all begun to gather dust, just a speckling really, but enough to see there isn't a lot of cleaning being done here.

The couch must have once been a vibrant red but is now dull with age. There are several stains on it that could be ancient or just a few days old. It's hard to tell in the low, yellow light emitting from a single bulb in the middle of the room.

As I am taking in the area around us, Art pulls away from me and quickly moves to the other side of the room. He crouches beside a sagging armchair where a frail woman is slumped with her head cocked to the side and her mouth hanging open as she takes shallow breaths.

"No, no, no, no, Ma ..." I hear Art pleading. The desperation in his voice shatters my heart, and I hurry to his side.

His hands hover over her. I wonder if he isn't trying to touch her because it would break his heart to find that he can't, or if he's afraid that he may be able to.

"What do I do?" he whines. He raises a hand close to her face but stops just before he would have made contact. "Ma, please."

His mom's eyes flutter open, glassy and red-rimmed. It takes her a moment to focus them but, when she does, they lock on Art.

"Arthur," she whispers in a cracked voice, like her throat is raw and parched. She slowly lifts an arm from where it was resting on the arm of the chair and wraps a trembling hand around his, which still hovered by her face.

With an incredulous huff, Art lets out the breath he was holding in and stares at her hand holding his. He places his other hand at her wrist and rubs his thumb over the back of her hand.

I look at her more closely and see that her skin looks ashen and wrinkly. Considering that Art was only twenty-two when he died, I would think his mom would be no older than late-fifties. She looks at least ten years older than that. It could be that she had him later in life, but this looks like age brought on by years of pain weighing her down. Concern for both of them sweeps over me, so I lay my hand on Art's knee in the hopes I can provide some sort of comfort.

Art's voice shakes as he says, "You can see me."

"And feel you," his mom says and lets out a contented sigh. "It's really you this time. My baby has finally come to take me home."

Art draws their hands closer to himself, unwilling to let go but needing to get her attention since her eyes closed again.

"No," Art says in a firm tone which she frowns at. "You can't come with me."

"Why not?" she asks. Her eyes fill with tears as she clings to his hand.

"What about Derrick and Lewis? What about the kids?"

"They don't need me. They're much better parents to those kids than I was for any of you."

"That's not true. Those kids love their abuela. And we love you, Ma. I wouldn't trade you for any other mother in the world. I wouldn't trade the life I had for any other life."

"I left you. A good mother would never have done that."

Art moves his hand from her wrist to wipe the tears from her cheeks which only makes her cry harder. He leans forward and places a kiss on the back of her hand still clutching his.

"You did, and I was angry at you because of it," he says. He wipes away her tears again as his words make her hiccup between sobs. "But I've finally been able to acknowledge that you were suffering too. Sure, you didn't handle it well. So what? We all make horrible mistakes. But are you really going to make that same mistake again? Because they do need you. They would be so lost without you, and they would feel guilty that they didn't help you. Is that what you want?"

His mom can only shake her head.

"Then call them, please. Let someone take care of you for once. It's okay to need that. We all need help sometimes," Art says.

She looks into his eyes for several moments before reaching for her phone on the small end table beside the chair. She pushes the contact for Derrick and places the call on speaker.

After a few rings, a tired sounding voice answers, "Ma? It's late. You okay?"

"No, Derrick. I don't think I am," she replies.

The voice immediately becomes sharper as the sleepy slur is replaced by concern. "What do you mean? What's wrong?"

"Haven't really been eating much lately. I may have lost too much weight. I'm just not hungry, and I don't want to get out of bed most days. When I do, I just move to my armchair. I don't know what to do anymore, Derrick," Art's mom whimpers. Tears flow faster down her cheeks, and Art continues to wipe them away.

"Ma, why haven't you said anything? No, no, never mind. This isn't on you. This is on me. I should have been checking up on you more often. I shouldn't have let you buy that little place," Derrick says. I can hear the panic rising in his voice, then I hear another voice faintly trying to soothe him.

The voice, which I'm assuming belongs to Derrick's wife, raises so Art's mom can hear. "Mama Elena, we meant it when we said you didn't have to move out. I know you wanted us to have the house, but there's enough room for you. The kids would love if you moved in. They adore you."

"I didn't want to be a burden," Art's mom says.

We hear of Derrick shuffling around—no doubt throwing on whatever clothes he can get his hands on and running out the door, and then he replies, "I'm coming over there right now, and I am taking you to the hospital. If they tell me that you shouldn't be living on your own, we're moving you back in, and I don't want any fuss about it." The shuffling stops, and he takes a deep breath before continuing, "I'm sorry, Ma. I'm not yelling at you. I know it's been hard for you. I should've stopped by more instead of calling. Just- I- I can't lose you too, okay? So, let me help, yeah? Don't try to do this on your own like everything else."

Her bottom lip quivers, but the tears have slowed. She nods, then realizes Derrick can't see, so she says, "Okay, Derrick. Okay. Calm down, sweetheart. I'm here. I'm not going anywhere."

There's a shaky sigh of relief then his voice again, "Okay. I'm leaving right now. I'll be ten minutes at most. See you soon."

"Drive safe," Art's mom says on instinct. "I love you."

"I love you too, Ma," Derrick says then ends the call.

Art's mom places the phone back on the end table and takes a deep breath.

"Thank you," Art says.

"No, thank you, Arthur," she says and pats his hand. Then, she's pushing herself out of the chair.

Art scrambles to his feet and hovers next to her, but she is steady on her feet. She waves him away and begins to shuffle to the hallway.

"What are you doing?" Art asks.

"Derrick is nervous enough as is," his mom says over her shoulder. "Can't have him seeing me like this. He's already prepared to take me to the hospital. I need to look at least a little presentable."

Art shakes his head as he watches her disappear into another room.

"Should- should we follow her?" I ask.

Art chews the inside of his cheek as he thinks then says, "No, but I'll check on her if she doesn't come out soon."

"She's still got some spunk in her," I say.

A smile appears on his face as he continues looking down the hall.

"From what I remember, she always did have an unlimited amount of energy. She must have kept some in reserve from back then," he says.

After a few minutes, she reappears and shuffles back down the hall. I see she's switched out her old, faded muumuu for a flowy sundress. She's also brushed her hair and possibly splashed some cold water on her face since there's a tad bit more color there now.

She scans the room. Her eyes pass over Art at first, but she turns back and squints at him. Concern flashes across her face, and she says, "Arthur, why can I hardly see you? Please, don't leave me just yet, baby." She reaches her hand out but can no longer grab him.

Art shushes her as tears begin to flood her eyes again. "It's okay. This is a good thing. It means you want to live. I want you to live too, so you have to let me go."

"I wanted you to come back, but I never thought of this part. Having to lose you again," she says through trembling lips, but managing to keep the tears at bay.

"We can say goodbye this time though," Art says with a sad smile.

"Oh, my baby," his mom coos. "I love you, and I am so, so sorry."

"I love you too, and I forgive you. Goodbye, Ma," Art says.

"Goodbye, sweetheart," his mom says and lets out a single sob as he apparently disappears from her view.

He takes a step towards the door, and her eyes don't follow him. He lets out a shaky breath as he watches her cry silently, still staring foreword at where he was a second ago.

I slip my hand into his, and he turns to me. There's pain in his eyes but also relief, and even a bit of joy. He gently pulls my arm to draw me closer and wraps his arms around me. I lift my arms to settle around his neck and knead the muscles there. His eyes stay on his mother, but I feel him relax against me.

"I'm really proud of you," I say.

He pulls away to look at me and smiles. "Thank you, Hannah."

I'm about to tell him he doesn't need to thank me when there is a rushed knocking at the door.

Art's mom jumps as she comes out of her daze. She takes a few steps toward the door when the knocking starts again.

"I'm coming, Derrick! Relax!" she calls out.

When she opens the door, Derrick takes her in his arms for a few moments before pulling back to inspect her face and weigh her frail-looking arms in his hands.

"Jesus, Ma. Have you been eating at all?" he asks, concern clouding every one of his features.

"Of course I have, Derrick. Not as much as I should, I can admit that," Art's mom says. "It's really not as bad as you're worried it is."

"You look sick," he says.

"I just haven't been outside in a while. Lost my glow," she says.

He shakes his head and sighs, "You been crying?"

She brushes her hands against her cheeks and says, "Arthur."

"We miss him too. You don't have to do this alone," Derrick says.

She nods, and Derrick takes her into his arms again.

Her eyes are still glistening when she pulls away, but no new tears have leaked out.

"You aren't taking me to a hospital tonight," she declares.

"Ma," Derrick sighs and rubs the bridge of his nose.

She cuts him off and continues, "It can wait until morning when the regular clinics are open. I don't need an ER, Mi Tesoro."

He stares at her, but she doesn't waver. Finally, he sighs and says, "Fine, but you're staying with us tonight." Not waiting for an answer, he stomps to her bedroom to gather some of her things, and she trails behind him, fussing that she can do it herself.

They reappear a few minutes later. Derrick is carrying the suitcase, and his mom is huffing along behind him.

"When we get home, I'm heating up a big plate of food for you, and I'm going to make sure you eat the whole thing," he says. He opens the door and motions for her to go first.

As she walks out, I hear her mutter, "All those years of forcing you to stay at the table until you finish your vegetables coming back to bite my ass."

Derrick chuckles and, as he turns to shut the door behind him, I hear him say, "Stubborn-ass woman."

Muffled through the walls, I hear her chiding him for the comment and can't help but laugh.

From behind me, Art's arms wrap around my waist. I feel his chuckles reverberating through his chest as I lean back against him.

He rests his chin on my shoulder, and I feel his breath on my neck as he says, "Thank you for coming with me. Thank you for helping me get to the point where I could come here."

I turn around in his arms to look up at his face. There's a peaceful smile on his face, and I can no longer detect that hint of pain sulking in his eyes I've glimpsed several times before.

"You would have gotten here without me, Arthur," I say and wrap my arms around his neck.

"I'm not so sure," Art says. He glances back at the chair his mother was sitting in, and his jaw clenches. "She wasn't doing well. You saw. I think I would have run out of time if you hadn't come along." He smiles down at me, but it quickly falls. He adds, "I'm not trying to say that I'm glad you died when you did. I meant—God, I sound so selfish—I just meant—"

I put my hand over his mouth and say, "I know what you meant, and you're welcome. But you've done even more for me. So, thank you."

I move my hand from his mouth to the back of his neck, revealing one of his dazzling smiles as I do so.

"You just helped me save my mom, Hannah. I can't think of what I've done to help you in a way as big as that," he says.

I look in his eyes and reply, "You've kept me sane. I would've been lost without you."

He caresses my cheek in his palm then pulls me into another hug.

"What now? We've still got some time before morning," he says.

"Hmm," I hum against his chest. Looking up at him, I say, "We could go back to the lake. Lay under the stars and listen to the crickets and frogs and owls."

"Sounds perfect to me," Art grins and nudges his nose against mine. His face changes as he gazes at me. It becomes thoughtful, also peaceful, and he says, "I'm so incredibly happy that I met you, Hannah King."

The butterflies begin wreaking havoc in my stomach again, but I manage to reply, "I'm happy to have met you too, Arthur Mancini."

He holds me closer, and I nuzzle my face against his chest. I feel his hand push through my hair to cradle my head.

I close my eyes and relax into his embrace, and we don't pull away from each other even when the silence of the empty house is replaced by the sounds of the lake.

20

Art and I don't automatically go to the courthouse in the morning. Instead, we wait until I feel the pulling in my gut that is becoming such a familiar feeling.

With Art's hand in mine, I let the feeling guide us, and we appear at the front of the packed courtroom. With the sentencing hearing held in open court, anyone could attend, and it seems like a majority of the town decided to show up this morning to see the final act of the drama that has taken up so much space in their minds for two months.

My mom is not sitting beside the prosecutor this time. She is in the first row behind the prosecution table along with Bobbi, her mom, and Julien. Behind her, I see Winslow and Dennis. She turns and thanks Winslow for all of his work that led to this moment. He leans close and doesn't glance away from her for even a millisecond. After she finishes, he nods in thanks, and a reserved smile flits across his face. He pats her shoulder and hands her a handkerchief which she dabs to her eyes. When she tries to give it back, he waves his hand at her to keep it as he leans back into his seat.

I'm surprised to see my dad in the crowd as well. He's in the first row behind the defense table. Whether his choice of seating is an intimidation tactic against Dale or if he only wanted to sit far away from my mom so as to not make a scene, I can't say for sure. Either reason fits his way of thinking.

In the sea of faces I catch sight of many people I recognize. Christine and Shelley are taking discreet pictures on their phones which they will most likely attempt to do during the entirety of the hearing, if they don't get bored and leave before it's over. My manager from Jimmy's sits with his wife who looks like she could start crying any second. He pulls out his handkerchief from his breast pocket, angles her face towards him, and dabs delicately at her eyes. They take a deep breath together, and she smiles at him. I spot several of my teachers along with some classmates and other people from the college I only ever saw in passing. I see many of my regulars from working the bar, all of them scowling, no doubt thinking of Dale and wishing the worst for him.

As I take in the sheer amount of people who showed up, whether in silent support for me or for curiosity's sake, the side door opens. Everyone's eyes lock on Dale as he is escorted in. Their eyes follow him to his seat and bore into the back of his head as he sits rigidly. Perhaps he wasn't expecting so many people to be here either. He seems to already be slick with sweat.

Shortly after Dale's arrival, the judge enters and takes his place at the bench. Once the opening formalities are out of the way, the hearing begins.

The presentence report is addressed first. The probation officer who put the report together goes through the content quickly but thoroughly. He states Dale had a near spotless criminal record before these crimes. His rap sheet only including traffic violations which he was quick to settle when they arose. The incident from my childhood is mentioned, but the officer points out that there was never a formal complaint made by me or my mother. Besides my mom, no one had anything overtly negative to say about Dale outside of his recent crimes.

The defense doesn't have much to say besides pushing for leniency when it comes to the sentencing and advocating for the chance for parole. They claim that the likelihood of him committing a similar crime in the future is next to none and lean heavily on the fact Dale has joined the congregation at the small chapel in the prison as well as frequently seeing the in-house psychiatrist. They say he is working diligently to process his guilt and find the root of the problem that caused this sudden tragedy.

The prosecution counters the fact nobody had anything bad to say about Dale with the fact nobody had anything good to say about him either. They also question the defense's claim it would not be likely for Dale to commit a similar crime if he were let out early on parole. They call on a psychiatrist to give their thoughts on Dale's crimes and what the likelihood may be of him committing them again if given the chance.

"This scheme to abduct and assault this young woman was born from and cultivated by an obsessive mind," the psychiatrist explains. "This obsessive nature was apparently kept at bay for a majority of the offender's life, perhaps he wasn't even aware of it before he found himself in the grip of it. He latched onto the victim early in her life. We've been told there was a previous incident which put distance between him and his obsession, a distance born of necessity not of any personal guilt from his actions. I've personally seen no evidence of Mr. Evans having a guilty conscious. The feelings of 'guilt' he refers to stem from being scrutinized and apprehended. He knows he is guilty and felt apprehension because of that, but it is centered around being caught as opposed to feeling remorseful. If there was never any suspicion around him, he would not have confessed. So, it would not be accurate to say the chances of him becoming a repeat offender are slim. All it would take is another obsession to take hold of his brain."

My mom takes the stand to make a victim impact statement, and it's the most heartbreaking thing I've ever had to listen to. She talks about the guilt she's been left with, believing she should have taken further action against him when I was younger. She talks about all the different plans I had for the future throughout the years. When I was seven, I wanted to be a dog trainer. When I was ten, I wanted to be a journalist. When I was seventeen, I wanted to be a forensic scientist. She wishes she had encouraged me to go to college for what I was passionate about instead of going for a business degree.

"Taking her from me has left me with a gaping hole that I can't help but fill with 'if only' and 'what if' thoughts that only torment me more," my mom says as she dabs at her eyes with the handkerchief Winslow gave her. "If I had only done one thing differently, maybe this never would have happened. Deep down I know it's not my fault, that it is Dale's fault alone, but she was my baby. I was supposed to protect her and watch her grow into the strong, successful woman I knew she had in her. Dale took that away from me but, more importantly, he took that away from Hannah. He took away her potential and all the good she would have done simply because he couldn't have her. Because of his selfishness, the world, at least for me, will always be dull."

I don't notice how shaky I've become from her speech until Art pulls me close, allowing me to sag against him. His arm around my waist becomes my support and my tether to the moment so I don't get lost in my mom's pain.

The prosecution finishes by questioning the importance of a previously clean criminal record. He argues, "Lessening his sentence solely based on his previous actions, or perhaps inaction, in turn lessens the severity of the vicious crime he has committed. If we were to be lenient with him because he was good in the past, we would be spitting in the face of every person this man has harmed with his most recent actions, Hannah in particular. He is facing four charges—aggravated assault, kidnapping, rape, and felony murder. These crimes were well thought out and executed ruthlessly which means he deserves every single year of his sentence, and he should serve it in its entirety. He didn't show Hannah any mercy, so what makes him deserving of our mercy?"

Lastly, Dale gets to speak on his own behalf. He takes the stand, and I really look at him for the first time since he arrived. His skin is pale and glossy under the bright lights of the court room. I even notice a bead of sweat drip down his temple and disappear into his growing beard. The hairs jut out at various angles or are gone in small patches from him tugging at them, which he does now.

He clears his throat into the microphone and begins, "I know there's nothing I can say that will undo the things I've done." His fingers untangle from his beard then begin tapping and picking at the wood of the stand. His voice goes through alternations of neutral and cracked with emotion as he continues, "What I did was unforgiveable, and I know I have to atone for it. I intend to spend every moment left to me in this life doing just that. I've been working with both the prison's priest and therapist to find what it is in me that brought about this tragedy, and I hope it will uncover answers that I can share with you all that will bring some closure and peace. I pray that I will have enough time to accomplish that, to do some good for those I've hurt. That's the most I can ask for."

I keep my eyes on him as he returns to his seat. His face remains contrite, lip trembling and eyes averted to the floor as he walks back to his seat, but the second his back is to the crowd, his face becomes blank. His fingers dig back into his beard to twist and pull while also picking at his cuticles on his other hand. He seems physically unable to keep still as everyone waits through the judge's short deliberation.

The judge keeps his head down, perhaps doing another quick overview of the evidence or looking over notes he may have made, then he turns his attention to Dale who is already focused on him. They stare at each other for a time, each most likely assessing the other in an attempt to ascertain the next move that person might make.

Finally, the judge speaks, "Mr. Evans, I'm unsure whether your strange demeanor throughout this proceeding comes from feelings of guilt or the discomfort of having the protective 'harmless man next door' shell striped away from you. However, it is not my job to psychoanalyze you. It is my job to take into account the facts of your guilt along with evaluating whether you may or may not be a further threat to society. Keeping in mind everything I have seen and heard today, I believe you to be a selfish and manipulative man. In my line of work, I've seen many men like you, and they often turn out to be the most dangerous sort of men. You are no different from any of them in my mind. I believe you would commit another act like this if given the chance, so I do not plan on giving you that chance. Come forward now, and I will read out your sentence for each charge."

With a guard flanking him on both sides, Dale is shuffled forward to stand in front of the judge's bench. Each crime is stated and explained before the sentence is given.

For the crime of aggravated assault, fifteen years on top of restitution paid to Julien for any medical bills as well as my mom for funeral expenses.

For the crime of kidnapping, another fifteen years.

For the crime of rape, thirty years.

The judge seems to get bigger after each sentence, building himself up as he reaches the final verdict. Towering over Dale, who now seems as small and inconsequential as a dust mite, the judge continues, "Lastly, you have been charged with felony murder, which is a murder committed during a violent felony. The court took into consideration your past criminal records, your admitted guilt, and the severity of the crime. The penalty for this crime is either life in prison, with or without the possibility of parole, or death. The court has examined all the evidence in this case, along with the circumstances surrounding them, and finds the sentence of life in prison without the possibility of parole to be most fitting."

I watch Dale's wilting stoicism crumble completely, not at the life sentence but at the judge's removal of the possibility of parole. I watch his eyes glaze over as he sees the rest of his life stretching in front of him and feels its bleakness in his soul.

With the final verdict given, the judge announces court is adjourned. Dale is shuffled back out the side door to the awaiting prison van, and everyone else begins to file out the main doors. Their chattering becomes loud and indistinct as every conversation echoes off each other in the cavernous room. However, I'm not concerned about any reaction other than my mom's.

She has come around to the prosecution table to profusely thank the lawyer, which he accepts with a hug before leaving for his office. Then, she is surrounded by her friends and receiving hug after hug.

When Winslow and Dennis come forward to congratulate her, she gives them each a big hug and tells them they are welcome to join in a small celebration back at her house. She says it won't last long because she will be flying to Colorado later in the day, but they decline as they have to go back to work.

They all leave together, and she says goodbye and a final "thank you" to the detectives as they split off from the group. Everyone else gets in the car with my mom and drive off toward home.

Art and I take the quicker, easier route, so we get there before they do. We appear in my bedroom. It hits me that this is most likely the last time I will see it. On the heels of that thought, this could also be the last time I'll see my mom. It is such a heavy thought I need to take a seat. I sink to my knees and sit on the floor.

Art sits in front of me and tucks my hair behind my ears so he can see my face.

"Are you alright?" he asks.

"Yeah, it's just … it's over now. So, today may very well be the last time I see my mom," I say and look into his eyes. I see an abundance of understanding there and realize he felt these exact same emotions last night.

"It's a hard thought, I know. I thought I had already accepted the fact I'd never see my mom again during the past two years, but leaving her last night was harder than I anticipated," he says.

"I'm so glad you were able to say goodbye to her," I say. I give him a genuine smile, but it falls too quick as I realize I may not be able to do the same.

Art guesses what's on my mind and says, "Hey, I bet we can think of something. You got pretty good at sending people signs. I know you can do it again."

I glance around the room looking for anything I could possibly use to send my mom a sign, to say goodbye and let her know how much I love her. But nothing catches my eye.

I sigh and lay on my back. I'm about to ask Art if he has any ideas when I spy a spot of color from the corner of my eye. Turning my head to the side to look under my bed, I find one of the discarded papier-mâché tiger lilies. She must have missed this one during her cleaning spree and hasn't noticed it since.

I extend my arm towards it but stop just short of touching it. I close my eyes and let the happiest memories I have with my mom flood my brain. With a smile on my face, I take a deep breath and close my hand around the stem.

I get to my feet and bolt for the door, calling to Art over my shoulder, "Quick, while I've got it!"

I hurry down the hall and into my mother's room using muscle memory as I keep my eyes fixed on the paper flower in my hand.

As I expected, my mom has her suitcase packed and ready to go lying on her bed. I place the flower on top of it and turn to Art.

"I can't believe I made it the whole way," I say.

He picks me up in a hug and spins me around, making me giggle. When my feet touch the floor again, I keep my arms around his neck and smile up at him.

"I've said it before, Hannah. You are amazing," he says.

Before I can think of a reply, the front door opens and the silence is broken by excited, chattering voices.

"Just in time," I say. Looking back at the flower, I feel a bit nervous.

Art must sense the shift in me because he squeezes my hand and says, "Don't worry, Hannah. When she sees it, she'll understand."

I squeeze his hand back and nod, but that's not what made me nervous. Now that it's so close, the anxiety I've been suppressing about passing over is rising to the surface. Saying goodbye to my mom could be the last hurdle. What comes next?

I press my face against Art's chest and relax into his arms as they envelope me. I focus on the calming feeling of his hand tracing slow circles at my lower back but perk up when I hear my mom's voice as she moves down the hall towards us.

"I'm just going to change into something else. This suit is stifling," she says.

"Well, that's no fair. I'd rather be wearing sweats too," Bobbi's mom calls after her.

My mom chuckles and replies, "You should have brought a change of clothes then."

She walks in, closes the door behind her, and makes it halfway to her closet before freezing in place.

Slowly, she approaches the bed and stares down at the flower atop her suitcase.

When she picks it up, her knees buckle, causing her to stumble against the bed. Sinking down onto the mattress, she doesn't take her eyes off the flower in her hand. Tears begin to spill from her eyes, but there is a smile on her face.

She looks around the room and whispers, "Hannah?"

A knock at the door causes her to jump.

"Ms. Carol? Is everything alright?" Bobbi's voice comes from behind the door.

"Oh, Bobbi," my mom says distractedly as she looks at the flower again. She shakes her head to clear her thoughts and calls out, "Come in."

Bobbi enters and notices both that my mom has not changed her clothes and has been crying. She immediately sits beside my mom and puts her arm around her.

"What's wrong?" she asks.

My mom brushes at her cheeks and says, "Nothing, actually. I came in here to change and found this on top of my suitcase." She hands the flower to Bobbi and continues, "I made a bunch of those to bury with her. I made them in her room and left a mess of them that weren't good enough. I thought I had picked all of them up."

It is clear that this was a discarded one as it is crumpled and a tad dusty. Still, my mom and Bobbi both look at it in wonder.

"I think she's saying goodbye," my mom says as fresh tears crawl down her cheeks.

"I think so too, but I think she's also telling you that she loves you and thanking you," Bobbi says, handing the flower back and rubbing my mom's back.

"Thanking me?" my mom asked. She shakes her head in disbelief. "What for? I failed her."

Bobbi frowns and says, "I think you know she doesn't see it that way. You were an amazing mother to her. You worked so hard to give her every opportunity possible for her. It was taken from her, but not from any fault of yours. What happened was in no way your fault. Keep looking at that flower and tell me she feels at all bitter towards you. She wouldn't want you thinking like this."

"I know, but it's so hard not to feel like I could have done more," my mom says.

"You helped put Dale in jail for life, Ms. Carol. Hannah needed that, and you were able to help give her that. I think she'll be able to move on now. Because you didn't give up," Bobbi says and hugs my mom tighter.

Bobbi lets my mom cry on her shoulder until the tears dry up. Then, my mom straightens up and looks at Bobbi with a tired smile.

"Would you like to say goodbye to her with me?" my mom asks.

Tears are brimming in Bobbi's eyes now. She blinks them away and nods.

My mom closes her eyes and says, "Hannah, I love you so much. I hope you are able to move on or rest easy now. I'll have horrible days and will probably cry myself to sleep most nights, but I will be okay, I promise. Don't hold yourself back for me. Go find out what comes next. I believe with all my heart that I will see you again. Until then, goodbye my baby."

Her lips graze the flower still held in her hand. She takes a deep breath, opens her eyes, and looks over at Bobbi with a wavering smile on her face.

Bobbi places her hand over my mom's and closes her eyes. After taking a deep breath, she says, "Hannah, I will always wish I had approached you sooner to reconnect. Maybe I should have let myself act like a crazy person like I wanted to in the beginning. Every night I wanted to call you and make you talk things through with me. Those 'maybe' and 'what if' scenarios will always be in the back of my mind, but I'll keep the good memories front and center. I'll always remember you and love you. I hope we'll see each other again. Goodbye, Hannah."

They sit together for a few moments in silence before another knock at the door jolts both of them from their thoughts.

"What's going on you two? Everything alright?" Bobbi's mom asks.

Bobbi and my mom brush each other's tears away with grins on their faces. My mom smooths down Bobbi's hair before she gets up and opens the door for her mom.

"Everything's okay, Jean. You two go on back to the living room. I won't be long this time," my mom says.

Ms. Jean looks like she wants to ask more questions, but Bobbi takes her hand and leads her back down the hall.

Alone again, my mom smiles fondly at the flower and kisses it once more before placing it on her nightstand.

As she continues on to her closet, I feel a tugging in my guts and reach for Art's hand on instinct. I see him already reaching for me as well. Our hands and eyes meet, and I can tell he feels it too.

"Is it time?" I ask him.

"Only one way to find out," he says with a nervous smile.

We both close our eyes and let the feeling guide us to where we need to be.

Even when I'm sure we've been relocated, I'm too nervous to open my eyes. Only Art's voice makes me crack them open when he whispers, "Hannah, you've got to see this."

Through the narrow vision I initially allow myself, I can tell wherever we are isn't alien in any way. I can make out trees, a blue sky, fluffy clouds, and of course, Art smiling down at me. So, I open my eyes all the way and take in the view before me.

We stand on a cliff near the top of the mountain overlooking the town. There are trees around and behind us, but the cliff ends abruptly about six feet in front of us. Below, the town is a collection of buildings the size of thimbles. We can't make out any people walking down the streets.

I begin to ask what we're doing here, when suddenly a light breaks through the clouds and expands forward like it's reaching for us. It's bright and warm like the sun, but it doesn't hurt to stare into.

And we do stare. We watch as it flows forward, stopping at the edge of the cliff.

"It's here," Art says and turns to smile at me. "Our way out." He moves to walk toward it, and I automatically reach out and grab his hand. I squeeze it apprehensively. He feels my hesitation and turns back to me with a reassuring smile. "Can't you feel its warmth? And not just that." He turns back to look at the light. His face a bit inquisitive, but still with a look of want as well. "It feels energetic. I feel so happy looking into it, like laughter is bubbling up in my stomach. It seems like it's reaching for me, to hold me. It's practically begging me to let it touch me." Again, he turns back to me. "Is that how it feels to you?"

It's my turn to stare inquisitively into the light. As I do, my anxiety about it slowly slips away. I ease my grip on Art's hand and say, "It's not exactly like you said. I do feel like it's reaching for me, but it feels more relaxed—more like it's asking me or cajoling me to accept it, like you would do with a stray cat. It feels understanding and accepting, but still ..." I look back into Art's eyes, which have not left my face the whole time I was staring into the light. "A small part of me is still scared of it."

Art moves so he's standing directly in front of me with the light at his back. Instead of acting as the sun would, casting him in shadow, this light illuminates him. He's glowing in front of me. The light makes everything about him brighter and sharper than anything or anyone had ever seemed before. I almost gasp from the sheer beauty of him.

He takes both my hands into his and looks me in the eyes. "Whatever there is for us in that light, whatever happens to us next, I know we will be together. Even if we're reincarnated, we'll find each other again." He moves one of his hands to my cheek and strokes his thumb against it soothingly. I close my eyes and rub my cheek against his palm one more time before he steps back, letting go of my hand and leaving only a faint feeling of phantom fingers on my cheek.

My eyes shoot open to see him walking backwards toward the light, still smiling at me.

"Wait," I whimper. He reaches out a hand towards me, but he doesn't stop taking those slow, careful steps backwards. He's getting closer to the cliff edge. "You'll fall!" I shout, and take a couple steps toward him.

"The light will catch us," he promises, and holds out his other hand towards me as well.

I look at him, both arms extended towards me, his hands waving me to come to him, his feet about to go over the edge. I start running to him. "Wait, don't leave me!" I shout, and plow into him just as he steps off the cliff. I wrap my arms around him and squeeze tight. His arms fold around me, and he breathes a sigh of relief in my ear as he nuzzles his face into my hair. Clutching each other, we fall into the light. It not only encircles us but flows into us as well, infusing us with its life-giving warmth.

Art maneuvers his hand under my chin and lifts it so I'm looking up at him. We stare at each other for what feels like an eternity, then he pushes his hand into my hair and cradles the back of my head as he kisses me.

It's the most mind-numbing kiss I've ever received. The only thing that matters is that we are together. All of my anxieties and doubts melt away. We open our mouths to each other and share our warmth. His warmth becomes my warmth. My warmth becomes his warmth. Becomes our warmth.

I feel now, stronger than I ever have before, that I will find Art again. I know that we will end up together because, in this moment, we are being made anew from the other's light. The promise of always will act as our beacons, drawing us to each other. We were, are, and always will be each other's lighthouse.

21

The light flares brighter until it's blinding, and Art is suddenly gone from my arms. I reach out all around me, searching for him, but he is nowhere near anymore.

Then the light begins to retract until it is merely a pinprick above me. I am being pulled towards it as if it is the source of gravity. I try to look down and around me in the hopes of getting one last glance of Art, but all is dark except for the light drawing me in.

It swallows me greedily, and I suddenly feel heavy and weary. My head pounds, and my body aches slightly, joints stiff as if from disuse. I take in a shaky breath as I blink my eyes fast in confusion, trying to make sense of what I am seeing.

It appears I am in a hospital room, but my vision is blurry as my eyes water at the assault of the lights above me. I rub at my eyes to clear them.

"Art?" I croak out from my parched throat.

I hear surprised intakes of breath and desperate shuffling to my right. When I open my eyes, my vision has cleared, and I see the face of my mother hovering above me with a look of pure wonder, love, and relief on her face. Her soft hands caress my cheeks, and her hair curtains around my head as she leans close to rest her forehead on mine. I breathe a sigh of relief as her scent surrounds me.

"Oh God, Hannah, we thought we'd lost you. I love you. I love you. I love you," my mom stutters through her tears and punctuates each statement of love with kisses to my cheeks.

"I love you too, Mom. Don't worry, you can't get rid of me that easily," I say. My mom lets out a sound between a sob and a laugh, and I follow suit. The laughter scratching its way out of my throat causes me to cough.

My mom straightens and presses the call button to summon a nurse.

"We'll get you some water right away, sweetheart," she says while stroking my hair. Her other hand rests against my arm and she holds it tight. Not uncomfortably so, but enough for me to know she is afraid that, if she were to let go, I may slip away from her again.

When I hear more shuffling, I realize my mom is not the only one in the room with me. On the other side of the room, Bobbi and Julien stand awkwardly next to each other. They both look hesitant to come forward, but Bobbi gets over her doubt quickly when I extend an arm to her.

She rushes toward me and enwraps my hand in both of hers. Her touch is delicate, but her face is even softer. She squats beside the bed to be even with my face as she gazes into my eyes, and I watch as tears form and spill down her cheeks.

"Stop that, both of you," I say to Bobbi and my mom. I blink hard and complain, "You'll make me start."

They both let out a short laugh, and my mom says, "We can't help it. We're just so happy."

I look back and forth between the two of them and say, "Me too. Confused, but very happy too."

There's a knock at the door before a nurse tentatively walks in, only to halt halfway through the door and stare in shock as my eyes meet hers.

"She's awake," the nurse states in wonder.

My mom's smile is the sun as she nods and says, "She needs water."

The nurse shakes herself out of her stupor and replies, "Of course, and I'll alert her doctor at once."

My mom isn't even through saying "thank you" before the door shuts behind the nurse's hurrying form.

I look up at Julien hovering behind Bobbi. His hands twitch and clench with nerves. I smile softly at him before looking back between Bobbi and my mom once more.

Shaking my head in bewilderment, I say, "I don't understand how I'm here."

My mom squeezes my hand and says, "Julien called the cops as soon as he got himself free. They were able to find you within the hour and rush you to the hospital for surgery. It was really touch and go for a while. Then you stabilized but you didn't wake up. It's been a little over a month."

My mind reels as I try to comprehend what this information may imply. I've been here in this hospital bed this whole time. Does that make it all a dream? And what about Art? Is he merely a fabrication? Someone I made up to keep me company in my state of isolation until I recovered? I don't want to believe that. I can't believe that. I felt Art's touch deep within my soul. How could that have been only in my head? And that question leads to a darker one. If it did turn out to all be in my head, then what about ...

"Dale," I exclaim in panic. "Did they get Dale?"

My mom is quick to soothe me. Her hand strokes my arm as she assures me, "They did, baby. John and Dennis, the detectives that worked on the case, kept after him from the start until they had enough evidence. He tried to run, but they chased him. That rickety old truck was never going to get him far."

I can't tell if I'm relieved or concerned her version of events doesn't entirely match mine. On one hand, it could mean a possibility that Art is still out there somewhere, hopefully alive and well. On the other hand, the discrepancies call into question almost everything I experienced. How could I get some details spot on yet drastically alter others?

"He was just sentenced to life in prison yesterday," Mom adds.

"Did he plead guilty?" I ask.

My mom looks at me a bit queerly for a split second before answering, "Not at first. He tried to go for the insanity angle, but the psychologists caught on immediately. That's when he caved and admitted to everything. Then he tried to play contrite at the sentencing hearing. I could have killed him myself."

The fire in her eyes tells me she would have if given the chance, and it reminds me of her promise in the graveyard. I can see that same righteous anger in her, but it isn't burning as hot as it was at the side of my grave. Another major alteration. Along with the memories of my wake. The list is growing longer, and I am growing more uneasy.

"Did Dad come?" I ask quietly. My meekness may come across as a jilted daughter clinging to a slim hope that perhaps her dad does care enough to run to her aid in a time of crisis, but in reality, it is because I need to know how many pieces I got wrong yet am afraid of the answers I may receive.

Mom glances up at Bobbi uncertainly. I catch a knowing and hesitant look pass between them, and the tension in the room pulls taut. Not the same tension, however, that I've felt countless times when anyone brought up my dad in front of my mom as I grew up. That was a smoldering tension, one that warned anyone sensitive enough to feel it that one more word could make the delicate string clinging to my mother's patience to snap. But this tension felt like everyone holding their breath in fear of spooking a cornered animal and causing it to act on its most primal instincts.

Mom's mouth opens as if to answer, but she is saved by the return of the nurse with a water bottle in hand and a doctor following in after her. The nurse glides in, hands me my water, and takes my vitals. Her movements are calm, almost soothing to watch, as she goes about tasks she's done day in and day out for who knows how long. The doctor, on the other hand, is a ball of energy, bouncing on the heels of his feet and clapping as he approaches my bed. He smiles exuberantly and holds out his hand for me to shake.

"Hannah, what amazing news to be surprised with today. I'm pleased beyond words," the doctor says. He's a short, stout Indian man with a smile that lifts his entire face and scrunches his eyes to slits. I take the hand extended towards me and it envelops mine completely. He places his other hand underneath our clasped ones and squeezes my hand in both of his. It feels nice, as his hands are very warm. I was unaware of the chill prickling my skin until he begins to thaw my hand in his grasp. He notices and asks, "Would you like me to get you another blanket? I'm Dr. Veer, by the way. And you are Hannah King. What a pleasure! How exciting!"

He claps again as he bounces out the door with a promise to be back with a warm blanket and to review the vitals Nurse Heather is monitoring.

Heather shakes her head at the closing door, but not in annoyance as there is a smile on her face and admiration shining in her eyes. She notices me looking up at her and turns her smile on me.

"Dr. Veer can be a bit of a handful, but he's one of the best doctors in his field. You have been in the best of hands, Hannah," she says, then returns to jotting down numbers and notes on her clipboard.

There are a few moments of comfortable silence interrupted only by occasional beeps of the machines I'm hooked up to and the sound of Heather's steady writing. Then Dr. Veer whirls back in to wrap me in a blanket that must have come straight out of a dryer. I snuggle into the warmth and await his verdict on my health.

He looks over Heather's clipboard with a serious face, smile gone and lips pursed—which is concerning at first, but he makes reassuring noises. He hums several *Mmms* and *Mhms* and relieved sounding *Ahs*. Then, he exclaims, "Excellent!" and hands the clipboard back to Heather. She nods in my direction and gives me a wink before she excuses herself from the room, her duties complete.

"You have recovered immensely, Hannah. Still, I would like to keep you here to monitor you now that you are awake. Plus, you will need a bit of physical therapy after having been motionless for a month, but you should be able to go home soon enough," Dr. Veer tells me.

He asks me to wiggle my fingers and toes, bend my legs and arms as far as I can, and roll my ankles, wrists, and neck. I tell him I do feel a bit sore everywhere, but I am able to do everything he tells me to.

"Very good, Hannah. We will try walking and doing more exercises tomorrow. Today can be for catching up with your loved ones. I have seen these three a lot this past month. They care for you deeply," Dr. Veer says.

My eyes begin to well up as I look at them all. I have another chance to love them like I should have. "I know how lucky I am now," I say as I choke back my tears.

My mom wraps her arm around my shoulders, squeezes me against her, and places a delicate kiss on the crown of my head.

After Dr. Veer leaves, another comfortable silence fills the room. Except I notice Julien is back to holding himself rigidly, fingers twitching, and biting his lip. I catch the quick touch of Bobbi's hand against his as she tries to soothe his nerves, but I think it makes him more nervous. I try teasing him like I always used to in the hopes that would loosen him up a bit.

"Julien, breathe. Stop acting like a frightened jackrabbit. You're making me tense," I say.

He lets out a huff of a laugh and finally meets my eye. He says, "Same old Hannah, huh?"

"Not quite," I disagree, but my smile grows. I look at my mom and Bobbi and ask, "Could you guys give us a minute?"

He gives Bobbi a nervous glance, but she squeezes his hand and walks out into the hall after my mom with the promise they will bring back loads of snacks from the vending machine.

With just the two of us in the room now, I beckon him closer. He comes to the side of my bed hesitantly with his head downcast and hands clenched at his side.

"Julien, seriously, what did I say? Relax. You and Bobbi ... it's alright. Honestly, it makes me happy," I tell him.

His head snaps up at the mention of Bobbi, and I can see tears have begun to spill down his face.

"Oh Julien," I whisper. Not really knowing how to comfort him, I reach my hand out to take his. He lets me, then he collapses into the chair beside my bed.

"I'm so sorry, Hannah. For everything. I don't understand how you can sit there and smile at me. I'm the worst," Julien says. His shoulders are hunched as he curls in on himself, not wanting me to see him cry.

"No, I'm the one who should apologize," I say. At this, he straightens to look at me. His eyes are full of confusion. I continue, "The way I treated you that night, and on so many other occasions, it was cruel and unnecessary. The truth is, I wasn't happy, but it had nothing to do with you. Julien, you are an angel, okay? I still care about you, I always did, but there was so much I didn't understand about myself and the things I wanted from life. I was confused and angry, but I never should have taken that out on you. And what happened that night, that was not in any way your fault."

Julien pushes the heels of his hands against his eyes as one sob wrenches its way out of his chest. Then, he rubs the tears away and nods.

Once he gets his breathing under control, he looks at me curiously and says, "Bobbi told me she came here the day after I kissed her. She said she felt so guilty that she needed to confess to you and that you squeezed her hand. The doctors told us at the start that you would probably twitch and move and maybe even mutter under your breath at times, but Bobbi was sure you were trying to reassure her."

"I suppose I was," I say after contemplating for a moment.

"You don't have any memory of it?" Julien asks.

"Not exactly," I say in a voice barely above a whisper. I'm lost in the memory of Bobbi at my grave, while I'm desperately trying to grasp an apple.

Julien seems to understand I either can't or don't want to expound on my cryptic statement, so we sit in silence until there's a gentle knock on the door.

"Come in," I call out.

Bobbi and my mom enter with three bags of chips and a Jell-O packet.

"We wanted to raid the vending machine for you, but the nurse said you shouldn't overdo it. She did give me this Jell-O for you though," Bobbi says.

As we sit together the rest of the evening, eating and laughing, a warmth blooms in my chest at how thankful I am to have them back and to be given another chance. But I can't help but feel the absence of the one person I want to see the most.

22

The next day starts my rigorous physical therapy routine, once they are confident I can walk on my own, that is. I'm shaky on my feet at first, but I get the hang of it quick and am able to begin physical therapy in the afternoon.

When I return to my room, I'm still sore but in a way that feels productive instead of feeling stiff. I take a hot shower to soothe the ache in my joints then settle into bed, planning to watch TV until I fall asleep. Except there's a knock at my door.

"Come in," I call out.

I'm expecting a nurse, but Bobbi walks in with a bouquet of lilies to replace the wilting ones on my bedside table. Laid next to the vase of real flowers is a bouquet of papier-mâché tiger lilies.

"Bobbi!" I exclaim. A smile spreads across my face, and I see it mirrored on hers. "You didn't need to buy me new flowers. I'll be breaking out of this joint soon enough."

She laughs as she finishes arranging the flowers.

"Well until then," she says, "you'll have fresh ones to liven the room up."

We settle into a comfortable stream of conversation as if we are picking up right where we left off so many years ago. Slipping back into our friendship is easier than remembering how to ride a bike after years of walking everywhere you go, and it's as comfortable as an oversized hoodie you can snuggle into when you just want to block out the rest of the world.

When the conversation reaches a lull, I ask something I'd been

wondering about since yesterday. "Bobbi, when I asked about my dad, I noticed the look between you and my mom. Did something happen?"

She hesitates but then nods her head and answers, "There was a weird incident. It was the only day your dad was here. A lot of people were in and out of here that day. That's when me and Julien met. We were here when it happened, and the two detectives were at the back of the room watching everyone's interaction with your parents. Anyway, Dale showed up and, when he hugged your mom, the vase of flowers on your table crashed into the wall there." She points at the wall across from us. Now that I'm looking, I can see faint scratches in the paint below the TV. She continues, "Your mom was excited, saying it had to have been you who did it, even though we know you didn't move an inch. Your dad was quick to dismiss her and to call you braindead even though the doctors told us several times your brain activity was normal. So, he almost got his throat slit by your mom brandishing a broken shard of the vase. Winslow was able to coax that away from her though. When she finally connected your possible tantrum with Dale being here, he was already gone."

My mind is a whirlwind again, but I ask, "Were there any other weird incidents?"

"Your mom thought she felt your breath on her neck once," Bobbi says. She also adds, "And apparently, when the detectives caught Dale, he told them that he saw you in his cabin one night and that he chased you into the woods. We assumed it was just part of his attempt at an insanity plea."

After several moments of me saying nothing, Bobbi asks, "Where were you, Hannah? Do you remember?"

I take in a shaky breath and reply, "I do remember, but I'm not so sure I could tell you where I was. Or when I was. But I wasn't alone."

Bobbi looks like she wants to ask more questions, but she simply says, "I'm glad to hear that."

Suddenly, I feel drained. The exercises mixed with my brain running around in circles has my eyes fluttering shut and my limbs feeling heavy.

Bobbi notices and says, "It's late. I'd better go so you can get some rest."

As she's slipping on her coat, I say, "Thank you, Bobbi. For giving me another chance. I've missed you so much."

"Oh, Hannah," she says and leans over my bed to pull me into a hug. "I've missed you too."

When we pull away, we both have tears on our cheeks. We brush them off each other with smiles on our faces and laughter in our eyes.

"No more of that, alright?" she asks. "Tomorrow could be the day you get to go home. Then, everything will go back to normal."

I'm not so convinced about the latter statement, but it does turn out I am released the next day. Dr. Veer is confident enough in my motor skills, and my vitals are consistent. So, by the end of the day, Mom is walking me to the checkout desk to bring me home.

"I didn't change a thing in your room, so you should be comfortable. I know you probably won't want to stay too long. You'll want your independence back soon enough. But I'm so glad you'll be home, Hannah," she says as we reach the desk where someone else and his mom are checking out.

I'm about to reply when the boy in front of us turns his head to say something to his mom. I get a good look at his profile and gasp.

"Art?" I ask under my breath.

"What's that, Honey?" my mom asks.

He heard me too. He turns to me and begins to ask, "Hi, do I kno-" but cuts himself off with a breathy, "Hannah?" He says it so low I would almost be doubtful that he said it at all if it wasn't for the knowing look in his eyes.

His mom turns around and says, "Carolyn!" Then, she notices me and gasps. "And Hannah! Oh, aren't our children miracles?" She pulls me into a warm embrace, and I wrap my arms around her in bewilderment.

When she releases me, my mom explains, "This is Arthur and his mom, Elena. I met her the night they brought you in. I was waiting for news about your surgery and here comes this kind lady, also waiting on news on her kid, but wanting to comfort me since I was a quivering, sobbing mess."

Elena waves her hand in the air dismissively and says, "I am no Saint Theresa, Carolyn." She turns her attention to me and continues, "Your mother needed a hand to hold, and I happened to have two to offer her."

"Oh stop that, Elena. She was my saving grace that night. I was clinging to her like a big baby. She was here because Arthur passed out that night," my mom says.

"Yes, Arthur had a brain tumor two years ago. Gave us such a scare. It was the size of a lime, but suddenly it shrunk. When they removed it, it was the size of a grape, and no cancer. Still, I was so scared when he collapsed that night, so I rushed him straight here," Elena explains to me.

I finally turn my attention back to Art, whose eyes I have felt on me during this whole exchange. I never could resist the pull of those eyes. I settle back into their warmth like I would into my favorite blanket. I can't hold back the sigh that slips past my lips as all the remaining tension in my body melts away under his gaze that feels as warm as a summer day.

"It's really nice to meet you, Hannah," he says. His hand extends forward, and I don't hesitate to wrap my hand around his. The touch is electrifying.

I hear Elena distantly behind the rushing of blood in my ears saying, "He was with me a couple times when I stopped by your room to check on your mom, but he was so out of it that month. The second he was through with all the scans and bloodwork, he'd collapse into a wheelchair and fall right to sleep. Slept nearly as much as you did this past month."

The chatter between our moms continue behind us but fade into the background as we simply stare at each other and clutch our hands together tighter.

"You're really here," I breathe out, afraid that if I speak too loud this reality may shatter around me and leave me alone again.

Art opens and closes his mouth a couple times, like there's something on the tip of his tongue that he's afraid to let out. Finally, he asks, "So, they weren't just dreams?"

"I'm not sure what it was," I say.

Art nods and takes a step closer. My skin buzzes at his proximity.

"I guess I don't really need answers. I'm just really glad we ran into each other here," he says. He's close enough I need to lift my head to look up into his eyes, and my stomach flutters at the memories that flood my brain.

"Maybe we could run into each other again sometime?" I ask. I wish I sounded more playful or sexy, but the desperate hope thrumming through me makes my voice thin and wispy.

"I'd love that, Hannah," he says. My name on his tongue sends shivers up my spine, and I can't resist the urge to lay my head against his chest again. He comfortably wraps an arm around my back and says, "Our moms seem to have bonded quickly. I'm not surprised since my mom could talk the ears off an elephant."

I chuckle and reluctantly pull away from his embrace to glance over my shoulder at the two of them laughing together.

"I'm glad they did," I say and smile back up at Art.

He graces me with one of his heart-melting smiles and says, "Me too. I'm sure they'll set up a play date for us soon so they can see each other again."

All of my relief and happiness bursts out of me as a laugh that is probably too loud for a hospital, but I don't care. I'm alive, and Art is entwining his fingers with mine as our laughter blends together in the air between us.

"I'm glad you're here, Hannah," Art says.

I wrap my arms around his neck and stand on my tiptoes to rest my head in the crook of his neck. My breath against his ear brings goosebumps to his skin and I grin.

"Me too, Arthur," I say and hold him tighter.